Seeking Miranda

The almost true story of a wretch like me

LINDA LEWIS

ISBN: 9798582050018

DEDICATION

To Drew Becker and the kiss that changed everything.

ACKNOWLEDGMENTS

Many thanks to everyone who read my blog, Shoes for an Imaginary Life in 2010, and encouraged me to write this book. 132,000 international hits were a vote of confidence like no other.

Prelude

Miranda watched as droplets of crimson and wine fell from the painting, its hues so saturated and juicy they were sweet enough to eat. At least that's what her imagination was telling her that day. In the painting there were three ladies seated at a table. The girl in front was the pretty one, her face turned away, her eyes averted. Was she shy, or was something else wrong? Miranda could see that even though the three were together, the pretty one was all alone.

Her companions were seated behind her. They wore ordinary dresses in muted shades that emphasized their stooped shoulders and plain faces. But the pretty one was a vision of loveliness in a long chiffon skirt. Its crimson and wine folds moved silently as she walked about. Her yellow blouse was sheer, a royal blue scarf draped over one shoulder. It had a design that looked like waves on the sea, placid and bright till a storm set in. Her clothes were adorned with painted flowers, some blooming, others starting to die. Because life is that way sometimes.

The pretty one had posture that was erect and without flaw. Her collarbone and long graceful neck gave her a regal appearance, even without a crown. The painting also revealed her small waist, shapely breasts, and a spritz of Chanel No. 5. Imaginary? Perhaps. But Miranda could sense things others could not. Her pale skin and lightly applied make-up were the perfect palette for painted ruby lips. Her appearance made her desirable, more than the girls seated behind her.

Even on Miranda's worst days the painting spoke to her. With all her nice shoes, and handbags, and good jewelry, Miranda couldn't help but wonder— could she be a princess, too?

The Castle

In the beginning, in the days before there were paintings, pirates, and too many cars, Miranda lived happily in a castle with a handsome prince who was smitten by her devotion, short skirts, and sweet silly ways. She traveled the world, wore pretty clothes, and bought shoes and handbags at her leisure. By kingdom standards, she was practically famous, or infamous, depending on who you believe. Naturally, Miranda had her faults, don't we all? But for the prince, with his Florida tan and winning smile, the skies were bluer when she was near him. Even after she ran away, left his side, and bound herself to disaster, she missed him dearly.

The castle had everything but a moat and a drawbridge. (In hindsight, some alligators and a man-eating shark might have been prudent.) The prince built it all just for her, designed it with Miranda in mind. As they watched their home take shape, they strolled through its vast rooms, climbed the spiral staircase, and walked all the way up to the place where the turrets touched the sky. Colorful royal flags would greet one and all! Miranda danced like a child as progress was made, singing silly songs in the wide-open spaces, listening to their melody's echo in return.

Spontaneous nights of passion were many, and the prince was happy to linger in bed awhile longer before starting his busy royal day. Some called it Camelot, still others scoffed at their age difference. Miranda called it small town pettiness. All the haters who said mean things were probably just jealous and wanted to be her. She looked so pretty in her diamond tiara, determined to never let her sparkle fade. She was certain that a shiny life would keep her happy forever.

Miranda set out to buy some nice things for the palace. Of course, there was her special painting, the Tarkay, the one with the ladies who brought both hope and despair. She bought expensive china— enough place settings to serve twenty— even though they always ate out. And on a summer trip to San Francisco, at a gallery by the bay, she spotted a life size statue of Neptune, King of the Sea! She knew the perfect spot in the courtyard facing the pool. With his severe appearance and pointed trident, Neptune could protect her and the ladies in the painting, too. He would rule over the lesser statues at his leisure. Miranda couldn't recall whether he was a good god, or a bad god, or any god at all. She hadn't kept up with Roman mythology since college. All she knew was that he was going to be a striking addition along her winding garden path, someone she would get to know well. Miranda found it curious that the prince liked him, too.

As the castle began to take shape, Miranda bought a 19th century Italian chandelier, forged out of iron with a million dancing crystals. It was pricey, of course, but when she imagined the imposing masterpiece hanging over her naked body in the garden tub, the crystal droplets painting a golden hue across her smooth skin, how could she resist? With the perfect lighting, her bathroom was fit for a queen! She imagined the prince coming home after a long day of ruling the kingdom. He would tell her about his day while she splashed around and teased him, motioning for him to join her. Most days he just blushed and turned away. The chandelier served her well; she had no regrets.

While Miranda was impressed with all her pretty things, it never occurred to her that the *real* God (not King Neptune), most likely was not. She didn't concern herself with religious matters, and always ignored the wisdom of the Palace Priests, even though they were both very nice men. Brother John and his brother, Brother James, worked as landscapers at the palace by day, and pastored a little church north of Providence on the weekends. Miranda could tell their faith was real. And she knew they cared about her. When she told them about the ladies in the painting and the colors dripping off, they seemed genuinely concerned. When she eventually ended up leaving the palace to move on, they gave her some parting words of wisdom and a small white Bible. There was a gold cross on the cover. It was shiny— she would keep it forever.

"Like a gold ring in a pig's snout is a beautiful woman who shows no discretion." Proverbs 11:22

Seeking Miranda

Cater to Me

Miranda spent money like a whirling dervish, a blaze of credit cards sliding and clicking. She loved the way glossy shopping bags felt against her skin! Her new Jaguar XJS was a surprise birthday present from the prince. As an extra touch, he had it painted to match her favorite lipstick, Max Factor *Red Passion*, long since discontinued, but she always kept a spare. The people of the kingdom whispered among themselves as Miranda drove by; hair flying, red lips glowing, her smile just a little too bright. No one realized how hard she worked to keep the prince happy! How dare they look at her that way! The car was an attention getter to be sure, with a Michigan license plate that read, K8R2ME. Was there anything wrong with wanting good service?

Being a successful prince, businessman, world traveler, and race car driver wasn't always easy. It took a lot of time and hard work. He was so smart about so many things, but it was more complicated than that. There were interest rates, stocks to consider, and parcels of land to acquire. With new Porsches to buy and a new boat every year, it was hard to keep the people of the kingdom all happy— and that included Miranda.

In spite of his fame, the prince had a way with people and the loyalty of the townsmen was true. He made old farmers in trucks feel important, made small talk with waitresses, and made his employees at work feel at ease. Girls wanted to ride in his car with him, and boys just wanted to *be him!* He was handsome yet humble, rich but never pretentious. He was good at telling bad jokes and never missed a punch line. Miranda wanted to be that way too, wanted to win people over and make them like her.

On weekends, the prince raced around the kingdom in his Porsche 930 (arctic white, big whale tail, always washed and waxed). It was a lot less flashy than the red one in the garage, and it made him look like a white knight on a tall white horse. When he drove by the people cheered! But Miranda noticed that even though his cars were fast and sexy, there were times when the prince seemed to be slowing down. The princess was just a girl, she didn't understand. He was under a lot of stress, and as his kingdom continued to grow, all his riches were at stake. If he leveraged one more business against another and things turned out badly, the world as they knew it could come crashing down.

Miranda feared for her pretty things. She did not understand much about business. But what she did know, was that she didn't want to live like a common person with one car and a shopping allowance. And she surely didn't want to become one of the frumpy women in the painting. She would give up the Tarkay before she let that happen!

In spite of her concerns about herself, Miranda was worried about the prince, the man she loved from their very first date. She reminisced about the fun she had getting to know him— it really was a funny story! She thought about the night he picked her up for dinner looking handsome as ever, dressed in a silk blazer, black T-shirt, and Italian loafers with no socks. She had on a short denim skirt, strappy Nine West sandals, and a clingy white T-shirt from her white T-shirt collection.

While the prince put on some opera music, Miranda riffled through her new Gucci Boston bag, (monogram canvas, brown leather trim with the traditional red and green cloth stripe). It was very grown-up with just the right amount of snob appeal— it was her first! A gift this expensive on a first date seemed like a bit much. She could only imagine the presents that were yet to come. Miranda took a pressed powder compact from her bag, powdered her perfect nose with the little cotton puff, and couldn't believe what happened next!

Out of nowhere, the prince *slammed* on the brakes. The car spun sideways, slid around a corner, and stopped so fast she nearly choked on her seatbelt! Before she knew what was happening, the prince jumped out of the car, ran around to the passenger's side, and lifted her out of her seat. For a moment she forgot all about retouching her make-up, noticed how big his hands were, and how nice they felt pressed firmly against her skin. He smelled really good, too. He stood her on the side of the road and said, *You must never put on make-up when you're riding in a Porsche!*

Oops, she thought to herself. Miranda made a mental note to never leave gum wrappers, french fries, Tic Tacks, or empty water bottles in his car. Or lipsticks, Sephora blotting papers, or coffee cups from McDonalds. Or used Kleenex, bobby pins, or extra straws in case the guy at the window screws up and forgets to give you one with your drink. She'd save all that for her old Toyota Celica, soon to be her former car in the blink of an eye.

The prince pulled a monogramed white hand towel from the trunk, (properly called the "boot," located in the front of the car), and asked Miranda to stand with her arms stretched out like a little airplane ready to fly. He dusted her off with the towel, front and back, while traffic slowed down to take a look. He rubbed the black leather interior until it was perfect and power free, placed her back in the seat, then drove off as if nothing happened. What might have been a learning moment, Miranda was certain was an isolated event. She liked to give people the benefit of the doubt. Those were such happy times.

But now, with the prince working so hard and feeling the stress of the business world, things had changed for the royal pair. The harder he worked the less she recognized him as the man of her dreams. He became depressed, despondent, and less interested in entertaining her— on the town, in bed, and otherwise. Miranda missed skiing in Aspen, schussing down the mountain in her flashy red snow suit. She wondered if they would ever again go swimming with the dolphins in Hawaii. She missed going on fancy business trips with him to lavish resorts where she could wear her good jewelry and her real Rolex, the one with the diamond dial. And she would never forget the trip to Jackson Hole, Wyoming, where there were plenty of fast horses but no Porsche dealers for several hundred miles. The irony amused her.

Miranda wanted to take another trip to the Opera de Monte-Carlo. The prince loved the winding themes of heroes and myths as the classic stories played out in song. Miranda's favorite was *The Enchanted Island,* an opera that was meant to be fresh and funny, but depending on your interpretation, had deeper meaning. She especially liked the part where topless nymphs in shear costumes surrounded mighty Neptune, reaching out to touch his robe, their arms moving gracefully like waves on the sea.

Long, thick snakes crawled up the girls' bodies, entwined with each other. While the prince studied his libretto to better follow the story, Miranda could feel the power of Neptune without reading a word. She hoped when they got back to the hotel, he would be in the mood for more than just talk. That was a grand night at the opera to be sure, but the prince was distracted. Unfortunately, no matter how much he had, the prince always wanted more. Miranda's appetite for nice things was the same. Their desires were toxic. It was a stressful time.

"Keep your lives free from the love of money and be content with what you have..." Hebrews 13:5

Miranda went shopping, he felt worse. She bought another Gucci bag, he bought another car. Then one night, tired again, he asked her to fix something for dinner at home. She suggested the Cabin Club was just a mile away, *close* to home. Miranda commented under her breath that this was not what she signed up for. She tried to hide her disappointment from her husband, then acquiesced and prepared a meal. At least Lean Cuisine Shrimp Alfredo wouldn't make her fat.

With patience and time, life as she knew it might have returned to "normal," but Miranda was in some kind of hurry, racking her brain for what it was she needed to be satisfied. She really did love the prince; she loved him from the first day they met, the first time he reached across the table at Red Lobster during a "business lunch" and touched her pretty hand. It was all innocent enough until he embraced her and kissed her in the parking lot. She could think of no one else. Like the lobster she ate for lunch and the melted butter that ran down her chin, he was hot.

Two years passed. The prince worked hard and life improved, but Miranda was restless. She couldn't put her finger on it, but she needed more. After careful thought,

Miranda asked the prince to give her the biggest gift of all. Not diamonds, rubies, not a yacht or a posh home on Ocean Drive. She had all that! It was something more beautiful, something lasting. She wanted the prince to give her a baby. The two would be bound in love forever, just like a real family! It was her first real desire to care for someone other than herself. More than all the treasures in the world, a baby is what Miranda wanted.

But there were issues lingering from Prince Charming's prior domestic situation, a marriage he left after that kiss in the parking lot. Making a baby would have required an operation to make it all possible, but he was willing. Sadly, the two could not conceive a baby the normal, romantic way. Miranda was devastated when they received the news. The doctor drew pictures on a tablet and gave them a detailed science lesson in anatomy, physiology, and the most advanced technology of the day, but offered little hope. No amount of money could change that.

It was Miranda's birthday, another year passed with little to show for her life besides more expensive jewelry and handbags. Or maybe it was because her disappointment was so profound, she could not openly share it with him. Either way, Miranda was heartbroken. She secretly grieved the loss of a family that would never be hers to embrace. Alone in her grief, she silently wept. The prince would have given her the moon, but he couldn't give her this. They never discussed it again. What a difference a baby might have made, especially in light of events yet to come. The ladies in the painting were in mourning, singing the words of a familiar song...

Lullaby and goodnight
With roses bedight
Lullaby and goodnight
Is baby's wee bed.
Lay thee down now and rest,
May thy slumber be blessed.
Lay thee down now and rest,
May thy slumber be blessed.

From "Cradle Song" by Johannes Brahms (1868) to celebrate the birth of a son by his former love, Bertha Faber. A hidden counter melody was written to suggest a song she used to sing to him, keeping discreet their love affair.

We all have our secrets.

Harry Stowe

Harry Stowe was everything Prince Charming should be— handsome, smart, funny, and surprisingly romantic for a middle-aged English chap. Harry Stowe was also very rich, and Harry loved Miranda. When she looked in his eyes she saw more than just dollar signs, she saw a mirror of her own beauty, her own worth. Unfortunately, she became so attached to her royal lifestyle, she hadn't considered who she would be if the reflection went away.

Harry was always beautifully turned out, dressed in crisp wool suits, silk blazers, and expensive shoes. When he leaned over to kiss her, he smelled faintly of soap, oak moss, and lavender. And when he sweated in the sun putting wax on his car, he smelled even better. His wavy blond hair was always uncharacteristically tousled for a man who wanted everything in its place. Harry had no idea how sexy he was— that was part of his charm.

Burton Stowe, Harry's father, was the first to admit that he spoiled his only son, the heir to his publishing throne. When he jokingly referred to Harry as *the prince*, the nickname just stuck. Miranda regretted that Harry's dad died years before they met, and liked hearing stories about how the two were opposites in many ways. Burton Stowe, Burt for short, was a curious man, a great adventurer who was always looking for a new hobby, something to invent, or a remote destination to explore. When he wasn't studying the annual raptor migration at Hawk Mountain, or cleaning his collection of antique firearms, he was inventing better lures to catch bigger fish. His publishing business was well staffed and had ongoing accounts that kept it profitable. Life was too short, and Burton Stowe was too wealthy not to indulge in some pleasure.

One cold weekend, Burt motored his old Chris Craft Sportsman to a secret cove. There were dozens of inland lakes near the town where they lived, and on that day he brought in a record catch while no one else was looking. He bought rounds of drinks for the crowd at the local pub, and served up a fish fry that etched his name in the town's colorful history forever. Even though Harry had a slight British accent (he loved to mimic his parents when they argued), he grew up in a big fancy house just outside of Providence, Michigan.

Sadly, when Harry's mother died, Burt spent less time at work, and more time chasing the happiness he once knew. He started to drink more. Like Burton, Harry Stowe was worldly and well-traveled, but took life more seriously. Whether it was in his work or the possessions around him, he liked things a certain way.

Harry carried a small level in his coat pocket and routinely straightened pictures around the house that weren't even crooked. No harm in that. His crisp white shirts were arranged in such a way that each one received equal washing and equal wear. Household staff knew better than to mess with the system because somehow he always knew. His boxer shorts were neatly pressed and on hangers, always worn in rotation for the same reason as above. Miranda hoped he never looked in her underwear drawer where a tangle of colorful panties awaited her each morning.

Perfect order was also maintained out in the stable, (a special name for a car enthusiast's big, fancy garage). Bottles of washes, waxes, Armor All, and sable detail brushes were lined up on chrome shelves, with the products arranged in rows like little soldiers, all facing forward so the labels would show.

Despite his reputation as a proper gentleman, Harry had an affection for the vintage girly posters that hung in the garage. The collection started years before when his father bought him his first car, (a used Porsche Speedster for his 16th birthday), and also his first sexy pin-up girl. It was an old-fashioned lady in a pointy bra on the hood of an Austin Healey Sprite. Miranda thought it was hilarious.

He had a poster of a pretty brunette in a short skirt, leaning over to change a tire with her underwear showing, and another of a long-legged goddess in black heels sipping champagne by a Jag XJS. It was the same car he bought Miranda for her birthday. She loved that Harry had a naughty side, as naughty as Harry could be. Sometimes she put on lacy underwear, stilettos, and red lipstick and climbed on one of his cars, waiting for him to get home. He gasped when he saw her fingerprints all over the hood, then gasped again when he looked at her. Miranda was happy being his girl.

She could tease him and get away with it because he knew her love was true. His wood paneled office at work was a study in compulsive neatness, with everything in its place. When Miranda stopped by to see him, she took great pleasure in moving some small object on his desk this way or that, holding her breath until he'd spot it, scoff, and put it back where it belonged. She grinned and giggled; his employees trembled with fear.

On his birthday, Harry was so surprised that Miranda baked him a cake— baked anything, for that matter— that he invited the staff to join him for a round of Happy Birthday. But when he blew out the candles and began to cut the cake, the room fell silent. The cake wasn't a real cake at all, but an empty box of Captain Crunch cereal, neatly frosted and decorated for the occasion. He rolled his eyes and kissed her on the forehead. Miranda could do no wrong, at least that's how it seemed.

When Harry took over the publishing company from his father, the business had been in a gradual state of decline. It was a small operation in a downtown store front. After losing many of the national accounts to competitors who worked to stay current, their most noteworthy product was a quarterly magazine for the Providence Michigan Orchid Society. Over time, Harry's charm and relentless efforts made Stowe Publishing a major force in the industry once more, with many of its periodicals printed in several languages, all of the finest quality. He was a proud, self-made man, with one fatal flaw: He was a rescuer of lost souls. He didn't even see it coming.

Just a few miles down the road from the castle, there was a little restaurant called the Cabin Club where Miranda and Harry sometimes met for lunch. The pub was of the old style, with an oak paneled bar and polished brass rails. Nineteenth century-stained glass reflected soaring colors, while whiskey bottles were arranged in perfect order.

They came for the food, the atmosphere, and to visit their favorite bartender Stella Wells, a lady who looked half her age and was putting two kids through college on the tips she made. She was quite lovely and did very well. Harry and Miranda sat at their regular spot and ate fillet mignon sandwiches with crumpled blue cheese and a salad. One day, whether by mistake or by fate, Stella poured two shots of tequila, Patron Silver to be exact. They were served with a shaker of salt and a quarter wedge of lime, a nice presentation with lethal consequences.

When Stella placed the drinks in front of a couple seated across the bar, the man said it wasn't what he ordered, he wanted something different. Rather than let the drinks go to waste, Stella offered them to Miranda and Harry. Miranda, a tequila virgin, was eager to try something new— lick the salt, down the shot, bite the lime, and wait to see what happens. She was feeling restless for no reason at all, and a buzz at noon on a Tuesday couldn't hurt.

"Wine is a mocker, strong drink a brawler, and whoever is led astray by it is not wise." Proverbs 20:1

Harry winced and politely declined, thanking Stella for the offer. But Miranda was quick to accept both shots. The prince never drank alcohol, at least not since the incident at Churchill Downs on the night of his fifteenth birthday. As he did every year of his youth, Harry met up with some of the other well-to-do boys, his eyes full of mischief.

On that day, when the adults moved out to the balconies to watch the race, Harry and his cronies drained every glass on every table, mint juleps and otherwise. Then he charmed the bartender out of a few shots more. He woke up the next morning in a horse barn, covered with hay and vomit, and badly hung over. A free shot of tequila, even from Stella, didn't interest him.

While Harry told his drinking story to the folks beside him, Miranda was levitating above the bar, buoyant and free, twirling her hair into a topknot and watching the party unfold. She could see herself hanging onto her husband, laughing hard, and talking way too loud. Could it be the tequila? While everyone else was confined to a wood and leather barstool, she was free to float along as she pleased, striking up conversations with strangers, and helping herself to the orange slices and cherries Stella had been arranging on a small platter. In spite of the lime chaser, the tequila's agave assault burned all the way down to her knees. She continued to hover near the prince and asked for another drink. Then somehow it was the next day, and it was morning.

Miranda popped two frozen waffles into the toaster and was about to take her morning pills. She tried to remember: *Did her doctor say she shouldn't drink alcohol with her thyroid medicine? With Lithium? Or an allergy pill?* Whatever it was, she would be sure to ask at her next appointment. Besides, she didn't feel *that bad.* It was just two drinks. And the next time they went to the Cabin Club, she was going to do it again. Harry couldn't stop her!

Judas

It was the end of the season on Lake Michigan. The clam bakes had come and gone, the boats on Grand Traverse Bay had all been pulled, and pirates were spinning tales of their thievery and charm. Fallen leaves swept through the parking lot of the Mallard Point Yacht Club, and the lake was restless, already preparing for her winter assault. Friends who had spent many fun-filled weekends together would once again go home to their respective towns. It was a summer to remember and the folks on the bar stools were drunk with beer and nostalgia— all but Harry, who disliked one particular person and couldn't wait for the party to end. The Michigan verses Michigan State game had the Spartans ahead by three at the half. It would be a long night.

A man called Judas sat alone at the corner of the bar opposite Miranda and Harry (who was, of course, not drinking). Judas was a grisly rogue with a full head of coarse red hair, a scar below one eye, and a gold pinkie ring. With a wolf-like countenance he was a predator in search of Red Riding Hood. Like his biblical namesake, he was known to be a man who would betray a friend. No one knew how Judas made his money. He claimed to be a Tier 2 supplier of electrical parts to a "Big Three" automaker. Some people took him at his word; Harry did not. His alleged frequent trips to Detroit made no difference— Harry smelled a rat. From Miranda's observation, he had many associates but few friends.

Miranda sipped her scotch, studying the viscosity of the strong drink in her glass. She sensed Harry's urgency to leave, and agreed to go as soon as she finished her cocktail. Without looking at the corner of the bar, she knew that Judas was watching her. It was like a children's book where the good person was warned not to look into the glowing eyes of the beast or they would be under his spell forever. But Miranda looked. She should have lowered her eyes and pretended to be searching for a lipstick in her Louis Speedy 30, a traditional Vuitton, her first. But instead she tempted fate, raised her head, and saw him sitting there— eyes aglow behind his bushy eyebrows. He was looking directly at her.

"The way of life winds upward for the wise that he may turn away from hell below." Proverbs 15:24

Sadly, it was too late.

While the others shouted and cheered at the start of the second half, Judas nodded at Miranda, silently beckoning her to join him. She knew she was putting herself in harm's way, maybe never to return. Harry would not be happy about this, but his strange allure was stronger than any resistance she could muster. He didn't smile or hug her goodbye as the other friends were doing. He simply raised his glass, toasting a summer past, and the memories that lie ahead. Beneath the bar he pressed a business card into Miranda's soft hand. Without looking at her he said, *call me.*

She raised her glass to touch his, and took a long drink until the scotch started to burn. She swore it would be their last exchange. Miranda waited one month; the business card lost somewhere in her crowded handbag. Then, on a dreary November day, she sat at her desk and watched the early winter rain come down. She stared at the phone then dialed. He had a surprisingly easy way about him; a charming conversationalist. He didn't seem surprised to hear her voice.

"Now the serpent was more subtle and crafty than any living creature of the field which the Lord God had made. And he (Satan) said to the woman, Can it really be that God has said, You shall not eat from every tree of the garden?" Genesis 3:1

A lunch date with Judas seemed like a nice idea, something neighborly, nothing more. Over drinks, he touched her arm, Miranda met his gaze and followed him. She wept all the way home. Miranda couldn't understand why it happened... why Judas took advantage of her that way! Never mind that she got a fresh manicure and wore a tight sweater under her business suit that day. There was nothing wrong with wanting to look nice, and it's not like Harry even noticed when she dressed up for him. He was always so busy with work, and so tired at night. Drying her eyes, Miranda looked in the rear-view mirror to see if she still looked like the girl Harry once knew… or if the darkness of Judas had somehow stained her, exchanging her formerly pretty face for a look of depravity like his own.

But Miranda was guilty. She said yes to Judas, to a lunch date in a distant town where she knew she wouldn't get caught. She said yes to a drink, to his breath on her neck, and a room at a hotel across the street. She wasn't even sure why she liked him— why she lingered with him that day— but she did. Judas fashioned himself the Pirate King, and enjoyed his reputation as the man with the longest yacht, the most money, and the biggest pirate hook. Though he promised Miranda their meeting would be kept secret, he couldn't wait to tell his drunken cronies and scallywags about his conquest. She was the pirate treasure he had been waiting for. Harry knew that Judas was a traitor— a scoundrel and friend to no one. Any girl among their summer friends could have fallen into his heinous trap. But Harry had no idea it would be Miranda.

The affair went on for months before she became careless and got caught. (Maybe she wanted it that way, who can say?) Harry retaliated with a vengeance and started taking away her prized possessions— the cars, her membership at the club, the priceless works of art she chose for their home. Pictures from their wedding and all their trips quickly disappeared from view. Harry filed for divorce. It was summer and all their plans were shattered because of her. Miranda was living in the east wing of the house and rarely saw her husband, but she was beginning to feel the sting of some very real consequences. Judas was a total jerk, no matter how much money he made! What was she thinking? How could she have even been with him? She would never speak to Judas again!

Jungle Red

Living under the same roof as Harry was painful. Staying in Providence wasn't going to make things any easier. Maybe she needed a change of scenery. Her phone was ringing off the hook with calls from Harry's rival. It was already late in the day when Miranda got an idea. If she wanted to leave town, she would need to book a flight and reserve a room in a hurry. Scanning her old-fashioned AAA atlas, looking from east to west, the only major coastal city she hadn't visited with Harry was San Diego. Without any concern for cost, without considering that it might be wise to sock away some cash for a rainy day, Miranda bought a first-class ticket, reserved a suite at the Sheraton, and started packing.

Her flight left out of Detroit in four hours. She hadn't told anyone she was leaving, not Stella the bartender, not her cleaning lady, and especially not Harry. She hoped he would be worried and try to find her. Miranda hadn't slept in days and her thoughts were spinning so fast she couldn't keep up with herself. The 737 landed with a bump in San Diego just before midnight.

Exhausted, drunk, and dehydrated from the flight, she took a cab to the hotel, checked in, and went to sleep. Miranda had a dangerous lack of fear when she traveled. The last thing she needed was to get lost, or robbed, or make friends with an unsavory man who could kidnap her and ruin her life— she already had one of those. In spite of her fears, there was one place she knew, one place that was safe and familiar. She woke up the next morning, showered, and put on a nice dress. Miranda was going shopping!

Never mind the ocean, the boats, the seaside dining. Forget the blue skies, the breeze, and the cute guys with surfboards. Miranda set out to find a lipstick that would transform her sorry mixed-up life, a shade that would put some sparkle into her despair. She took a cab to the mall, went straight to Sephora, and sampled several shades on the back of her hand. Miranda chose Nars Jungle Red; a highly pigmented shade, a little dry, but able to go the distance. It couldn't hurt.

She bought a shiny retractable lip brush at MAC and a pair of tall sexy sandals at Nordstrom. Who knows when a girl might need them for a night on the town? She left the mall, tipped the cabby, followed the boardwalk back to the hotel, and passed by a window covered with pictures of boats for sale. A handsome man around her age came out of the office and asked if she'd like to go aboard any of the listings. She picked out a beamy 1969 41-foot Hatteras, a lot of boat for a girl. He raised one eyebrow; she assured him she could handle it.

"So tell me about the boat. How many hours on the engines?" She gathered up the hem of her dress, climbed down into the engine room and asked whether the twin Detroit diesels had been pressure tested. The fiberglass was dull and oxidized, but otherwise the boat was in pretty good shape. Of course, she would want a professional survey if she decided to make an offer. Miranda would love to have a boat of her own. Kevin McGregor, yacht broker extraordinaire, grinned. He loved boats and so did she.

They walked the docks, went aboard some others— a Bertram sport fish, a late model Sea Ray Sundancer (almost a million dollars) and a 1947 61' Trumpy houseboat. Miranda gasped. It had been fiberglassed above the waterline— something a knowledgeable boat owner would never do! She emphatically told Kevin that a woody had no business being in salt water in the first place. Did he know what that would do to the value? The sea air had badly damaged the original fittings; the chrome on the brass cleats was badly pitted. Miranda shook her head, lamenting the future of that stately old beauty if it stayed in the ocean.

"This boat belongs to the Great Lakes, someplace like Mallard Point or Little Traverse Bay." Those waters were full of priceless wood boats— the Garmins, HackerCrafts, and lapstrake Lymans. The boats were so full of history and life, the old dockmasters considered them family. She told Kevin about the beauty of Lake

Michigan, how she could look off the swim platform and see the bottom at thirty feet. Miranda was unaware that she was preaching to the choir. Kevin raised an eyebrow, curious about a girl in a dress who wanted to talk about engines and fittings. He asked Miranda if she would like to discuss it over dinner.

They went to a small, trendy bar and grill a block off Fifth. Miranda ordered the Mahi Mahi with a side of wasabi mashed potatoes, and a gooey chocolate dessert. She was never a salad and Pellegrino girl. She sipped a scotch and made it last through dinner, while Kevin had a tall, imported lager. It's not that Miranda had a drinking problem. She simply didn't want to get drunk or sleepy while she was having so much fun. Also, her new shoes looked great, but the heels were so high she had to be sober to walk in them.

Kevin invited her to join him for a boat ride the next day. He was entertaining two men and their families for a midday cruise on the boat they just purchased. The new owners, two brothers, were growers and packers of vegetables whose labels you see on grocery store shelves every day. They were among the wealthiest families in Mexico and would be chartering the boat south to Cabo San Lucas when the last of the paperwork was complete. How could she say no?

"Wisdom, like an inheritance, is a good thing and benefits those who see the sun. Wisdom is a shelter as money is a shelter, but the advantage of knowledge is

this: that wisdom preserves the life of its possessor." Ecclesiastes 7:11, 12

It was a beautiful day for a boat ride on San Diego Bay. The men brought along their wives and a handful of well-behaved children. The weather was ideal for a cruise. While the women and children were not fluent in English, watching the kids play aboard their dads' gleaming new ship brought smiles to everyone—laughing children, the universal language.

Once outside the bay, their friendly gathering was interrupted by Captain Kevin. He motioned for Miranda to join him at the helm. His cheerful expression was uncharacteristically grim. One of the engines had failed. He said it wasn't unusual to encounter a few minor problems the first time out. In boat lingo it's called a shake-down cruise. However, a boat this size needs both engines to maintain control and stay on course.

He asked Miranda to take the helm, turn the boat, and head back to the bay. She was sober at the moment—thank God— trying not to drink until five. She took the controls and knew she must remain calm. Kevin headed for the engine room, keeping his composure as he walked past his guests. Time was of the essence. *Why was Kevin gone so long?* Miranda had been running boats since she was a kid, but not anything the size (or price) of the mammoth Italian yacht, the resplendent Ferretti 870, nearly 90-feet long.

The passengers were terrified when they saw Miranda at the controls. Women in their culture weren't the take-charge type; many of them didn't even drive. She got the feeling the men liked it that way. Miranda's "crew" could be of little assistance since none of them had even been on a boat before! She tried to remember all the things Harry (and some other boating friends) had taught her when they bought their new boat and motored it from Bay Harbor to Grand Traverse Bay.

Throttles on boats all operate the same way, using them to control speed in the open water, but also for turning and maneuverability at slower speeds. If she had to dock this thing with one engine it would be a nightmare. Miranda had taken down her share of uprights in her day, part of what she considered the learning process. Now was not the time to tempt fate and do it again. The rules for navigation are the same everywhere, too— *red, right, returning.* As long as she could spot the buoys, she could find the channel. The adrenaline rush raced all the way to her toes... *I can do this.*

The trouble was in the fuel line. Kevin returned to the helm, radioed that he would need help at the dock, then motored down the channel at idle speed with one engine, the bow thrusters, and a steering wheel. The Ferretti made it safely into the dock where their adventure began. Kevin's skills as a boater and technician amazed her. His command of the situation made him very attractive. Miranda stopped to look at her phone and ignored the call from Judas— again. She was beginning to see that she was worth more than that.

The brothers thanked her profusely for her "heroism," which she dismissed, insisting she was just glad to help out. The eldest of the two handed her the keys from the ignition and said in a gracious tone, that she was welcome aboard the yacht anytime during her stay in the city. It was a fabulous offer, and the men seemed honorable and sincere. But she politely declined.

Miranda needed to think about going home, then silently wondered whether a divorce could be completed via fax or email. She didn't want to have to face Harry. On the flight home to Detroit, Miranda wrote in her journal, reflecting on her amazing adventure. She spent a lot of time with Kevin McGregor. He was a great guy, successful, and very handsome, but never made a move on her. She decided he must be gay.

The Marinette

The divorce was uncomplicated. Harry had the papers drawn up while Miranda was gone. She knew when she signed the prenup that she and Harry would always be together. What kind of girl in her right mind would screw up a marriage to Prince Charming? She signed the documents against her lawyer's advice and received nothing but a mere pittance, an insult really. All she wanted was the painting.

Meanwhile, Harry kept a low profile and handled himself with character and integrity, but that didn't stop every pretty girl in the kingdom from chasing him. The most interesting complication that arose was the sale of the couple's boat, a 60' motor yacht called, "Seeking Miranda." She and Harry had so much fun at the lake every weekend, watching the boats come down the channel, and sipping cocktails at the club after dinner (except for Harry, of course, who was not drinking).

Their dockmates knew from the way they looked at each other that the two would be together forever.

Miranda was unsure of what her future would be like all alone. She had some money in the bank. She had a college degree. Maybe she should get a job and rent an apartment. Those were surely all possibilities, but Miranda was more interested in excitement, drama, and mayhem. She wanted to live life on her own terms for once! There was an old aluminum boat, probably not safe to board. A prospective buyer for "Seeking Miranda" wanted Harry to take it in on trade as partial payment for the Stowe's boat.

It was a faded hardtop, poorly maintained, and according to Harry, ready for the bone yard. But Miranda had an idea. She asked Harry to accept the deal— she wanted that boat! This wasn't San Diego and the boat was no Hatteras, but she saw real promise in this venture. Harry had been around boats his whole life. He was an expert. And while Miranda was good at the helm, she was no welder, craftsman, or engine mechanic... or carpenter, plumber, or electrician... or a professional who could replace a fuel tank or refrigerator. Miranda decided to restore the old boat anyway. She wanted to make her like new again.

It would be expensive, but Miranda knew where she could get the money. The check she got from Harry each month was barely enough to survive, at least not the way a princess should. She felt her blood run cold, a chill crept up her back. Strange, she thought. It was a warm October day. The exterior work would have to be done first, and it needed to begin right away. Winter was coming. But then the solution came to her. The next time Judas called, she would answer.

"As a dog returns to its vomit, so a fool repeats his folly." Proverbs 26:11

Miranda stayed on at Mallard Point and moved aboard the old boat, scrubbing her way through grime, old sticky messes, and bad smells from decades past. Someone even managed to spill a bottle of pink nail polish on the toilet seat— a tacky shade, no less. Water was running brown out of the galley spigot even with a freshwater hook-up. The cabin lights flickered when the wind blew. She was no electrician, but she knew that couldn't be good. If there was any money left over, she would hire someone to do a complete electrical upgrade, maybe once she made it to Charlevoix. She would ask around and find somebody good.

The first night aboard, she lowered the table in the little dinette into the sleeping position. It would be a temporary bed until the cozy v-berth was clean and ready. Removing the stench of little kids sleeping in there, eating candy and wetting the bed at night would take some time, and stronger chemicals than she had on hand. There were still so many unknowns about the boat, and safety was a big concern.

As it got dark, Miranda's courage started to fade. She was exhausted, dirty, and craving a drink, but didn't have so much as a beer in the fridge. It was dirty, too.

She decided to sleep with her clothes on— jeans, Michigan State t-shirt, and sneakers. If there was an emergency she would have to act quickly. On that note, she climbed on top of her sleeping bag and turned out the light. She kept a fire extinguisher in bed beside her, and a long metal flashlight next to her pillow, just in case. The water lapping sweetly against the old hull was reassuring.

Miranda stared at the ceiling, thinking about Harry, the way she ruined her marriage, and a few other lonely thoughts— bad thoughts about Judas. Then she saw something move— something small. She squinted to see it... *slowly crawling in the shadows.* Adrenalin seized her! She jumped up, grabbed the flashlight, tripped over a shoelace, and ran off the boat. Spiders would be moving indoors now that the cold weather was here. And Lake Michigan spiders were the worst. Not deadly, of course, but big, and hairy, with a bite that would leave welts and a rash forever! They say once you were bitten, you never forgot. Miranda was sure it was one of those spiders. What else could it be? Thank God she spotted it and got out when she did.

In the morning Miranda woke up in her car, sore and hungry, but happy that in spite of the emergency, she was still alive. With a renewed sense of courage, she climbed aboard the old boat and stepped down into the cabin to take a look. There were no spiders anywhere to be seen. But on the spot where the giant spider once stood, there was a small round screw head that kept the headliner in place. And at regular spaced intervals there was another, and another. Her spider was hardware?! She swore she saw it move, but without her glasses on who could be sure? More than a little embarrassed, she vowed to tell no one. It was the first of many secrets.

A transformation had begun. Old stainless-steel cleats and fittings were stripped from the boat's faded topsides, cleaned, and polished. There was a second chance, something good waiting beneath all the cracked paint and oxidation. Screens were replaced, leaks were sealed, things that were broken were repaired and made new again. Miranda worked in solitude, preferring her own thoughts to the conversation of curious visitors who dropped by to stare at a dust covered girl with a power sander.

Boat work was demanding. Most days Miranda woke up while it was still dark, skipped a shower, and headed out to the McDonald's on Mallard Point Road. She bought the local paper for a quarter, took her place in line at the drive through, nodding at the tradesmen and marine workers who were starting to be familiar. She opened her wallet, looked down at her hands. They were rough and raw, with yesterday's paint still stuck underneath her fingernails. She had the hands of a charter captain, but didn't care. These were signs that her hard work was paying off. The project was on schedule, she hadn't fallen in the water or gotten hurt, and she was staying on budget, thanks to the money from Judas.

"Hey..." she shouted, a smile in her voice. The line moved forward and Miranda spotted someone she knew.

The bearded man in the truck ahead of her rolled down his window, lit a cigarette, and shouted, "Hey yerself'!" Her boat restoration had created quite a stir among the locals, especially those in line at McDonald's who she solicited for free advice with breakfast each day. "Did you roll and tip the topsides the way I told you ya should? It always looks real nice on aluminum." She heard him order three Egg McMuffins with extra ketchup and a large coffee black.

The roll and tip method is one the old timers at the lake swear by. It saved Miranda around $6000 by doing it herself. She had been painting all week while the weather was good, and the results were stunning. By laying down an even distribution of paint with a sponge roller, then lightly smoothing the surface with a brush till the roller marks don't show, she got the appearance of a professional sprayed finish for the cost of the paint.

"I finished painting yesterday, and the boat looks like new!" For a girl who never cleaned or painted a day in her life, Miranda was amazed by how much she liked hard work. She thanked him for his advice, got her coffee, and moved on.

Seeking Miranda

Tommy' s Gotcha

The decision to leave Traverse City was both an emotional and a practical one. While Miranda's fondest memories of Harry were there, she couldn't stay at Mallard Point forever. The exterior work was nearly complete. Lake Michigan was getting colder and more threatening by the day. If she didn't leave Traverse City the boat would have to be pulled, winterized, stored, and launched in the spring. It would cost too much money.

Instead, she would make the run out to the end of the Leelanau Peninsula and spend one night in the town of Northport. If she had mechanical trouble or ran into weather along the way, she could always duck into Sutton's Bay, roughly the halfway point on the first leg of her trip. The next morning, she would get an early start and head north to Charlevoix. She found a marina that would bubble the boat and allow her to dock and live aboard there until spring. Miranda put on her leather boots and grabbed her Louis Vuitton Petite Noe. It was a bag designed during Prohibition to carry around Champagne without getting caught— not that Miranda had anything to hide. She headed straight for Tommy's Gotcha, the bar where everybody knew her name.

Tommy's was an old, converted storefront that was originally a business office for the adjacent campground; after that, a greasy spoon that served breakfast all day. Though not exactly welcoming on the outside, the oak paneling, cozy bar, and ceiling fans gave it a certain appeal. More than two hundred polished brass pressure gages covered one wall, a collection started by Tommy and made famous by customers who kept it going.

Booths with red upholstered seats were mended with duct tape, and the old linoleum floors had seen better days. She once told Tommy his bar wasn't "bag worthy," suggesting it was a place where an expensive handbag might rest on something dirty, be touched by a child with sticky fingers, or accidently bumped by a stranger. He grumbled and installed brass hooks under the bar so her good bags wouldn't get scuffed or dripped on. Entrees started at $22.95, salads and side dishes were ala carte. You'd think at those prices Tommy would replace the furniture— but probably not.

Tommy Blum was everybody's favorite bartender, confidant, and after-hours drinking partner— a mensch in the truest sense of the word. Tommy was old— *had always been old*— but just how old, no one knew. Every year in June he celebrated his 70th birthday. The party originally started as a small intimate gathering (when Tommy was 70), and had grown into a festival bigger than the Grand Traverse County Fair. There was a beer garden, a band (this year, a rare performance by Pat Benatar), and a huge inflatable gorilla in the parking lot. If people didn't stop to join the party, at least they beeped their horns and cheered.

Tommy was a matchmaker, a heartbreaker, and a dream taker depending on who you asked. He kept tabs, kept secrets, and stashed his money in a desk drawer at the end of the night. Tommy did not believe in banks. He was skilled at managing the restaurant's finances and knew all about business affairs. In fact, he knew about tax right-offs that most people hadn't even heard of yet! He was a small operator, he once told Miranda. The IRS didn't care about the little guy. He passed on advice and sound, motherly wisdom but personally ignored both. Girls who came into the restaurant already drunk and acting foolish were written off as Mishuginas, but encouraged to stay anyway. Crazy girls were the best marketing tool a man in the restaurant business could hope for, Tommy once told her, and it sure worked for him.

Conversely, customers with coughs, cold, or flu symptoms were sent home to drink a nice hot gorgle morgle (an old family recipe of whiskey, honey, and who knows what else)! He did not need sick people leaning on his bar and spreading their germs all over the help and paying customers. His joint was a money maker, not a walk-in clinic. Miranda didn't have a therapist in those days, but she had Tommy, and she was his favorite crazy girl— less like a date (he was seventy, after all), more like a grandpa. He amused her with stories of his military service, and talked fondly of his work as a munitions instructor during the Battle of Las Vegas.

Those were busy years for Tommy, especially since he was running the sports books, and dating several beautiful girls all at once. (Even at age seventy, Tommy Blum was a lady's man and always had a pretty young girlfriend with a free drink in one hand, and the other in his pants.) Miranda reserved some pages in her little black address book and took it out of her purse to take notes whenever Tommy started speaking Yiddish. She was determined to learn enough to keep up with him, but mostly to honor their friendship. When she told Tommy everything that happened with Harry, he took her hand and calmly said, *"bashert." It was meant to be.* What Tommy really meant was, he already knew the whole story because Judas sat at the bar and talked about their affair in detail.

Tommy knew Miranda was leaving in the morning and poured her a scotch straight-up, a double Macallan 12-year, smooth, not too smoky— a nice going away present on the house. Tommy never gave free drinks to anyone— not even Pat Benatar. Most of the regular crowd had gone for the season, except for Vince the imaginary cowboy, and his fearless sidekick, Buster. Buster had so many DUI's his license was suspended for life plus forty. Maybe they would finish their drinks and leave on a horse together.

The town's best defense lawyer, Joe Ramono, sat a few seats down from his potential clients, a fat cat in a fishbowl. Miranda sat on a bar stool next to Joe and hung her bag on the hook. He greeted her with a pleasant nod. They were acquaintances but not quite friends; Joe was very private. Directly across the bar there was a couple she didn't know. The girl was Miranda's age but with more wrinkles and too much make-up— certainly not very becoming for a lady. She had had too much to drink. The man was older and very handsome, apparently her date.

He had a striking appearance— long silver hair pulled back into a neat ponytail, and thick black eyebrows with a prominent arch. Even though he seemed to be having a good time, something about his countenance made him look angry. His eyes were so blue, she caught herself staring. The man wore a navy blue blazer, conservative tie, and shiny cuff links at the sleeves. She noticed he was wearing a ring, gold and prominent, but not on his left hand. He was unseasonably tan for November— looked like he probably smelled good, too.

The man in the navy blue blazer was having a good laugh with Tommy. When he ordered another drink, Miranda detected an accent. When she asked Joe Ramono about the man, he took a long drink of his beer and shrugged his shoulders. Information from a lawyer is never free, and besides, she would never see the man again anyway. *Too bad,* she thought. She needed to stay focused on her journey, no sense flirting with him now. The drunken girl was lucky to have him. Tommy shouted last call, and there were friendly good-nights all around. How Vince and Buster made it home safely was always a mystery.

The next morning, Miranda climbed out of her v-bunk, turned on the blowers, and opened the hatch. She leaned into the musty engine room and smelled for gas, then turned over the ignitions, warmed up the twin 454s, and made one last check of the items stowed in the cabin below. Her power tools, circular saw, and heavy orbital sander were packed securely in a storage area beneath the dinette. A dozen quarts of oil, a six-pack of fuel filters, her paint, tool belt, and several rolls of R-19 aluminum-backed insulation were secured in boxes, ready to be installed before the bad weather hit.

On deck, inside the wide aft bench, she stowed her dock lines, plus 200 feet to spare, a boat hook, a net, and a Bible in a zip lock bag— the one from Brother John and Brother James, the Palace Priests as she fondly remembered them. As a rule, no one gave Miranda presents unless they wanted something in return, but these men were honorable. On the day they gave her the Bible and wished her well on her journey, it meant a lot. They would be happy to know that she read it sometimes and tried her best to figure out the meaning, hoping it might help her somehow. John said, "We'll pray for you, Miranda." The boat kept her busy, but her direction was lacking.

"Men will stagger from sea to sea and wander from north to east, searching for the word of the Lord, but they will not find it." Amos 8:12

She would miss the Mallard Point Yacht Club. She knew that once she left, she would never come back, not only because the cost of the membership and dues would be far out of her league, but because all of her friends there were enemies now, every tie had been broken. She doubted that Harry would be back either. Miranda looked at her watch. Twenty-five nautical miles traveling at 14-knots meant if she left Mallard Point by noon, she could be at Northport in two hours, give or take.

She tapped the engines in reverse, back to neutral, back in reverse to let the nose come around. She understood good boating practice and seamanship. Miranda pulled out of her dock, leaving Mallard Point with a heavy heart and quiet seas ahead. There wasn't a single red lipstick in sight, only a half used Chapstick that she could apply without looking. She hugged the shoreline all the way to the end of the peninsula, wondering if the man in the navy blue blazer might be a boater, too.

Miranda reached Northport a little ahead of schedule, and saw the rickety old docks ahead. She backed off the throttles and drifted at idle speed till she got her bearings. She would go close to shore and dock into the wind. With a tap of the starboard engine... then another... then back to neutral to let the stern come around, she threw a spring line onto an old wooden upright. The weather had failed her, it was getting cloudy. Just as she wished someone would have noticed her docking the old Marinette like a pro, she saw a man out in the cold, waving from the parking lot. Miranda breathed a sigh of relief. The wide-open waters of Lake Michigan were more than she could handle alone, and she knew it. When she left for Charlevoix in the morning, Judas would go with her.

Charlie Fine

Of course his real name wasn't Judas. His real name was Charlie Fine— president and CEO of whatever he actually did for a living. But he didn't credit his business success to his education or work ethic. He attributed everything to good luck. The mysterious gold ring, the marbles, special coins he carried with him, the silk good luck charms, and other trinkets were, for some reason, more significant. He was an eccentric, chain-smoking alcoholic, and Miranda liked him. And hated him. It was complicated.

The way Charlie managed his social life was another story. He earned his despicable nickname by chasing pretty girls all over the Great Lakes, and deceiving their husbands into thinking they were all just friends. When Miranda called and asked if he would help run the boat up to Charlevoix, he was thrilled! They would spend the night on her boat and leave Northport at sun up when the lake was its flattest. Charlie loved adventure. And in spite of everything that went wrong when they were together, he was crazy about her.

Miranda thought about the day she took possession of her boat, how she walked round and round with a clipboard making notes. When she realized how much the restoration would cost, she called Charlie and asked him to meet her. Deeny's Hideaway was a discreet little bar and grill outside Traverse City, a few miles past where Mallard Point Road goes back to two lanes. It was a neighborhood tavern frequented mostly by factory workers, fisherman, and lonely housewives. Liquor was cheap. As much as Harry Stowe loved to buy things, Charlie was tight with his money, preferring bar whiskey to premium brands, and sometimes suggesting they split an entree or an appetizer. That seemed a little odd to Miranda, but he was known to be an unusual man, very private for a pirate, never married all these years. She didn't question his weird ways.

Deeny's Hideaway had two pool tables where men drank beer, played for money, and ignored calls from their wives. When the after-work crowd went home, younger women, flirtatious and tan, came in for drinks. Sometimes they stripped down to their swimsuits, did jello shots off each other's bellies, and passed out on the pool tables till morning. These were Charlie's "friends." He often suggested they could be Miranda's friends, too, but she politely declined. Charlie's appetite for sexual adventure had no bounds, and he was not shy about asking people to join the party. In his imagination, Miranda always played along.

Miranda had been to Deeny's before. But on this particular day, the day of their "business meeting," the bar was closed. A handwritten note on the old screen door said the owner, Deen Jr., had to leave due to an emergency. That usually meant he forgot about a court appearance, was running from a sheriff's deputy with a subpoena, or hiding from the mother of one of his babies needing grocery money. Deen Jr. was a colorful character.

"Hey, darlin'..." Charlie was leaning out the window of his old black Volvo when she pulled up, mumbling past a cigarette in his mouth. There were no other cars in the gravel lot. The smell of his cigarette smoke was intoxicating. Miranda could never figure that out. "Not sure what kinda trouble Junior got himself into this time, heh, heh... but we're gonna need to come up with another venue. I hear you're real excited about that new boat of yours." Miranda was just waiting for him to suggest they go back to his boat and have a drink. She would simply say no and suggest someplace else... perhaps the new Bob Evans out on Route 6.

"Y'know, I haven't pulled the boat yet, and it's a heck of a lot nicer and cleaner than this place. How 'bout we just go back to Mallard Point and you can tell me all about your plans to start the restoration. I'm proud of you, Miranda, ya know that, don't ya..." Although she hated him, she knew he meant it. It was a Thursday. He was always at the lake on Thursday when the club was deserted, then stayed on through the weekend. Miranda would go back to his boat, have one drink, and show him her proposal with estimates for completing the job.

She followed him from Deeny's down Mallard Point Road, paying extra attention to the place where the road narrowed to two lanes. There were still orange barrels and caution signs even though the road was supposed to be finished. She followed him past the storage building, around the clubhouse, and out to the end of B-dock. Miranda knew that as she slowly approached his boat and drove past the giant potted geraniums, a wireless motion detector would send a signal to a receiver at the helm, which would in turn relay a signal to the antique Chelsea clock in the main salon causing it to chime twice. Charlie liked to know who was coming and going. Even when he wasn't at his boat, he got a notification on his phone, including the times they were in a hotel room alone.

His boat was simply called, *HOOK.* If there were an asterisk and definition at the bottom on the transom it would say, *a curved or angular piece of solid metal or other hard substance for catching, pulling, trapping, or suspending; something that attracts attention or serves as an enticement.* Miranda was once a dove caught in his pirate snare, a partaker of his curved, hard, substance—but no more! She climbed aboard willingly, but this time their meeting was strictly business.

They walked across the gangway, took off their shoes, and climbed aboard. Charlie's boat was a maze of whimsy and mischief, rare collectibles, and pirate treasure. There were polished mahogany cabinets and furnishings with plush white carpet— Captain Hook meets Hugh Hefner. Miranda *loved* Charlie's boat. There were sensors, blinking lights, and surveillance devices all over the place. Miranda took Charlie's word that there were no video cameras on board— anywhere.

There was a well-stocked bar with an impressive row of crystal ships decanters, and some narrow vertical shelves where Charlie kept his maps, journals, and photos from his travels. Most boaters just hung out at the club and got drunk all weekend; many never left the dock. But he traveled the Great Lakes with abandon, piloting his own yacht, many times all alone. It was on an occasional Thursday night that Charlie taught Miranda to run and maneuver his boat. The club was quiet then. He was delighted but not a bit surprised by how adept she was at handling the longest yacht in the harbor. *Red, right, returning,* he shouted, as she brought the boat in from the lake and down the channel. He was an expert, just like Kevin McGregor, but that is not why she was on his boat that day.

Charlie surrounded himself with beautiful objects, women and otherwise— gold coins and nautical antiques, some of which he swore were owned by actual pirates, and some that he swore were *magic!* A colorful display of authentic Japanese Omamori were framed and hanging opposite the sofa where Miranda was seated. The detail in the colorful silk designs was stunning, and promised to bring the owner good fortune.

She once asked Charlie about his ring, a heavy gold signet ring with an image inscribed on it. It looked like the three-pronged weapon held by the Neptune statue at the palace, and also the one at the opera. He never took it off, not even when they were in bed together. When she asked what made it so special, he wouldn't say. Maybe Charlie Fine thought he was King of the Sea, too!

Charlie watched Miranda reach for a familiar painted box, secured by an ornate clasp. She opened it, careful not to spill the contents, and began sorting through the antique marbles inside. She was looking for the ones that were her favorites— the ones she liked to hold in her hands and roll around till the cold glass turned warm against her skin. Miranda looked inside and caught her reflection in the mirrored lid. She twirled her hair and checked her shiny lip gloss.

Something about those marbles always made her relax, though she could not say why. Miranda took a deep breath and noticed Charlie watching her. It was the same look he had on his face the night he gave her his business card at Mallard Point, the night she looked into his beastly yellow eyes and couldn't look away. He sipped his drink, took a long drag on his cigarette, and flashed a familiar grin. Charlie liked to be amused— and that's one of the things he liked best about Miranda.

"Go ahead, Miranda. I know which marbles are your favorites... the ones that give you the most pleasure..." He chuckled a pirate's chuckle and offered her another drink. Miranda cleared her throat and took out some papers from her bag. Charlie bought it for her on one of his business trips— a traditional Chanel flap bag, black caviar leather with a gold chain handle. She always carried it when she was with him. He had excellent taste for a bachelor.

Charlie looked over her plans, the materials list and labor costs, and said he was impressed. He would set up accounts in her name at West Marine in Petoskey, Lowes, and the corner hardware store where she could get the supplies she needed. They would be paid in full each month, and she could keep buying more. He offered to open similar accounts at Nordstrom, Saks, and Victoria's Secret, but she declined. It was bad enough that he was bank rolling the restoration. She didn't want to owe him anything more than she had already given.

Miranda was daydreaming, playing with the marbles, looking at their pretty colors instead of at him. There were carnelians, amethysts, and a single sulphide marble with a tiny lamb figurine inside. She reached her hand to the bottom of the box, twirled it around, and found one of the two rare antique German Indian marbles, black and shiny with a wave of bright colors. Sometimes their bold presence spoke to her, made her wish she was stronger. She wondered about the ladies in the painting, her beloved Tarkay. She missed their company, their wisdom... hoped she would be with them again one day. Miranda sorted through and found a banded lutz, a rare clambroth marble, and a hand painted China marble that didn't seem to fit in with the rest of the collection, but Charlie liked it anyway.

There were several mysterious core swirls which she set aside, then turned them loosely in her hands. The orange and yellow marble was the sun coming up over a new day, the way it looked from the aft deck when she and Harry got up early and sat outside with their coffee. That particular marble always made her feel hopeful that things would get better, that Harry might want her to come home. Her favorite green swirl was the most complex, with ribbons, and streams, and bits of confetti inside— a tropical garden in a ticker tape parade. She smiled, aware that Charlie was still watching her, and decided not to notice. She could feel his "magic" trying to seduce her, but his efforts would be wasted on her that night.

She gazed into the box, moved some aside, and picked up another one with special meaning. It was a brightly banded core swirl in shades of crimson and wine, its hues so saturated and juicy they were sweet enough to eat. She picked up another, turned the marble in her hand, then stopped at the place where ribbons of cobalt and capri opened to form a gradually deepening pool. Sometimes she thought about going inside, sinking, falling into the cool water and letting the swirling colors take her down. The marbles gave her peace.

"Take one, Miranda. How 'bout that crimson swirl you always find... or maybe it always finds you," he laughed. "That would be the magic in it, wouldn't it now." Charlie had never even met the girls in the painting. How could he know? She declined, said she knew it was very valuable and didn't want to break up his collection. What she really meant was, she didn't want to have that connection with him— not even a stupid marble— when she started her new life alone. Once she finished the restoration, she had no plans to see him ever again. But now was not the time to explain that. She handed him the crimson marble, grabbed the money, escaped his kiss, and ran!

It was starting to rain at Northport. Miranda secured her lines and adjusted the fenders to protect her new paint job from the splintered wooden uprights and the wind. She looked up and spotted Charlie leaning against the abandoned marina building with wind burned cheeks and hair blowing madly. Charlie called out her name and waved. She ran to the end of the pier to meet him; he kissed her cheek. As usual, he smelled like cigarettes— a filthy habit she reminded herself, yet a strange appeal that made her want to forget about the weather and take him to bed. He was pushing a loaded marina cart full of gear. Miranda liked getting presents. There were three electric space heaters, plastic jugs for hauling water, and an OSHA approved first aid and safety kit. He brought two CO2 detectors (one for the bilge), a Garmin GPS, and night vision infrared binoculars. Miranda was excited— this was like Christmas!

There were flashlights, floodlights, and a portable generator. There were fuel filters, gaskets, and a spare propeller— brand new and shiny! Charlie believed in being prepared. There were big batteries, medium batteries, and two dozen double A's. "I know you'll be thinking of me, heh, heh, heh." There was a wrapped package stuffed inside a small shopping bag. It caught her eye. He told her to look inside. It was a small round box, very old, covered with fine embroidery in shades of teal, periwinkle, and gold. Inside there were a dozen marbles, all her favorites.

"It's to remind you that even when I'm not here, I'm still thinking of you." He smiled a warm smile. "So that's pretty much everything you'll need to get started, except... "He looked at the back of the boat, his eyes flew wide open. "Miranda! There's no name on the back of your boat!! Darlin' you promised me... YOU PROMISED!!" Charlie believed that running without a boat name was bad luck. But he believed marbles were magic, too...

The scar under his eye was more noticeable than usual. Miranda hoped Charlie didn't think that just because he gave her the money to restore her boat and some shiny marbles to play with, that she was interested in renewing their relationship (or whatever he called it). They climbed aboard the old Marinette to get out of the wind. Before Charlie took off his coat, he reached for an inside pocket and showed her several stacks of bills, still in the paper wrappers. Miranda looked away and whispered, *thank you.*

She told herself this was classic Stockholm Syndrome, a bizarre psychological condition whereby a fair maiden (like herself), over time develops positive feelings for the pirate who captured her, stole her innocence, and carried her away. She began to see the gifts, the trips, the jewelry, and all the money as expressions of his affection. The line defining their association as an *arrangement* verses a *relationship* had become blurred. She could only imagine what the Palace Priests would say about that? Although she was no scholar, and certainly not playing by the rules, she knew the Bible was clear on certain things. But she was in so deep, there was no escaping now.

"A prudent man sees evil and hides himself, the naive proceed and pay the penalty." Proverbs 27:12

At the Charlevoix Boat Basin, Miranda wrote in her journal:

I'm so excited to finally be here! It was cold and windy coming up the lake...even hugging the shoreline it was rough. We didn't lose an engine and nothing down below broke, spilled, or caught on fire. Charlie was his usual confident self, but once we got out on the big lake he insisted we put on life jackets. Winds out of the south are the worst this time of year. I could have never made it by myself.

So here I am, my first night at the Boat Basin, Bizet's "Carmen" playing sweetly through the stereo speakers I installed all by myself. In the story, Carmen wonders who will own her body, as she recalls the men who are fighting for it. Harry loved the opera, Carmen— Charlie thought she was a stripper. In the morning I can hook up the TV, sign up for cable, and organize my CD's. That should keep me entertained when the cold weather hits. And there's always that little Bible. Some of the things I've read make good sense, but most are easier said than done. Charlie left as soon as we got the lines set. I'm exhausted... glad I don't have to entertain him tonight.

"Free yourself, like a gazelle from the hand of the hunter, like a bird from the snare of the fowler." Proverbs 6:5

The lights on the water are festive... reflections of the lights on Bridge Street. Checking the chart, there's supposed to be a Coast Guard Station off to starboard and a red channel marker 4/s off to port. It was dark when we came in... plenty of time to look around in the morning. Jack's Steakhouse is just above the marina, and I can see faces in the windows looking out... an audience watching a play, a story about to begin.

I'm choking back happy tears wondering if all this is for real. Charlie keeps pestering me about naming my boat. He says I should call it "Snow White" *since I'll be out here all winter. I keep telling him that I don't want to spend the next five months listening to bad Seven Dwarf jokes, or looking like a dealer selling cocaine. Anyway, I have a better name in mind.*

Tomorrow will be busy. I need to look into an electrical upgrade, get a price quote on shrink wrap, call the cable company, and find a good sign man. I should make a chart of my amperage usage so I don't blow a fuse or start a fire. I need to find a liquor store and refill some prescriptions, too. I've been out of medication for a month, but I feel fine... I really do. If I were manic, spinning out of control, I would know it... of course I would! But now I'm heading up to Jack's Steakhouse, ready to join the game, ready to meet the players.

Seeking Miranda

Seeking Miranda

It was cold but clear when Miranda bumped into her new neighbors on the dock the next morning. "Nice boat. So what do you call her?" asked the tall one. Naming the boat had really become an issue.

"Are you kiddin' me? You call yourself a boater and you don't even have a name?" said the short one who had a voice like a foghorn. "That aluminum raft is gonna be your best friend about two weeks from now... so let's get on the ball and get her done!!" He sneezed and wiped his nose on the back of his hand.

"It's important to be able to identify yourself and your vessel in case of an emergency. We're just thinking about your safety." The third man had deep brown eyes and a quiet voice. She imagined he was probably very handsome, that is, if she could see him. These were Miranda's new dockmates, Sneezy, Grumpy, and Bashful. They were dressed in matching Carhart's and worn Sorels, with black ski masks pulled down over their faces.

Miranda was wearing a white parka with a real fur hood, skinny jeans, and her good Enzo boots. She was probably a little overdressed, but how did she know she was going to run into three of the Seven Dwarfs out on the dock that day? It wasn't even that cold. They looked ridiculous.

"Of course my boat has a name," she said. "Didn't you see me dock when I came in yesterday? I'm pretty sure I nailed it when I sterned in on the first try." (It was too dark to see that it was actually Charlie at the helm.) "So yes, I am a *real boater,* and yes, my boat will have a name! I know you were watching from Jack's Steakhouse when I came in!" She was baiting them. "I've been waiting for an experienced sign and decal man to lay it out for me. I would never want anything but the best for my raft." She sneered.

"We'll hook you up with Captain Brad... he's the best. He does everybody." They laughed hysterically like college boys at a frat party. She knew the type. "And when you meet Brad, what will you tell him? Do you have a layout? A drawing? A clue? Seriously, Miranda... we're all friends here. We want to know..." *She thought for a moment... definitely not Snow White, or Ice Princess...*

"I'm calling her "*Seeking Miranda.*" The sound of it warmed her heart. She knew all along that would be the name, but saying it made it real. Miranda smiled and said, "The letters will be gold and shiny with a bunch of diamonds on one side and a red lipstick on the other. Happy now?"

"It's gonna be a long winter... a girl with red lipstick and a bunch of diamonds peein' in a coffee can." The short one was going to be a problem.

"Yeah... a coffee can. This I gotta osee."

She watched them from the bar at Jack's Steakhouse the night before. She was sure they saw her motor in. How many boats pull into the Boat Basin just weeks before winter? Miranda did not introduce herself, but instead took a seat at the bar to watch. She didn't want to interrupt the waitress as she delivered another round of Pabst Blue Ribbon to their table. Better to observe them in their natural habitat to see what she was getting herself into.

As long as there is a lady's room at the marina, there will not be a coffee can on board unless it's for making good coffee! Miranda had considered her winter wardrobe and knew there would be more L.L. Bean than Victoria's Secret, although she had already purchased some cute panties and matching bras just to get her adventure off to a nice start. She would prevail against the elements just like the guys, only prettier.

Miranda already bought a type III life vest to wear on the docks (not curve enhancing but very safe), strap-on ice cleats, and boots from Canada with steel toes and real shearling liners. They made her feet look huge! And then there was her glamorous red snowsuit, the one Harry bought for her in Aspen. She added a soft Polartec neck warmer and a trapper's hat with ear flaps. It was made of real fur!

People from her old life— especially Harry, Charlie, and Brian— would never believe this. Somebody better take pictures— she looked fabulous! Her fashion show was interrupted by a loud knock on the bow. "I hope you're down there working on a drawing for your aft deck superstructure and not admiring your outfit." *Oh my gosh... is that idiot watching me!?* "We're not going skiing, Miranda, and this isn't the bunny hill. We're here to *work!"* He whistled.

It was Ron, the tall man on the Hunter 36, the sailboat on the dock directly across from her. He had been a winter boater at the Boat Basin the longest. Since his divorce he had no interest in playing house, alone or with anyone else. Ron drove a car carrier, delivering cars from the Ford Plant to dealerships all over the U.S. He asked permission to come aboard, took out a handkerchief to wipe the fog off his glasses, and turned down Miranda's offer for a drink.

They sat comfortably at Miranda's little dinette; the bench seats still upholstered in dated turquoise vinyl. Ron explained that as the temperature dropped, it would become more difficult to keep the inside boat temperatures livable, even with the most powerful space heaters. Just as boats that are pulled and winterized get shrink wrapped for the season, winter boaters would need to do the same things, not just for protection from the wind and snow, but to keep themselves from freezing.

A superstructure skillfully designed and crafted from PVC plumbing material would create a strong frame to support the sturdy vinyl covering. It would provide a huge, enclosed area the same dimensions as the aft deck, and would be essential for storing extra supplies, tools, and emergency gear. It would increase the interior temperature by at least ten degrees without any further insulation. A poorly designed superstructure, on the other hand, would blow away on a windy day, doing significant damage to her boat, and creating a hazard to everyone living on the dock.

She looked at Ron's finished drawings, expertly laid out to scale on graph paper. *Well crap. This is going to be really hard. Maybe I should use some of Charlie's "emergency money" and hire an architect, or...* Ron handed her the tablet, a protractor, and a ruler and said, "Welcome to the dock, Miranda. Knock on my boat if you get stuck. I can give you a hand."

"Two are better than one, because they have a good return for their work: If one falls down, his friend can help him up." Ecclesiastes 4:9

She thanked Ron and followed him into the dark, cold night to make some preliminary measurements. Charlie's floodlight made her aft deck as light as day. Miranda heard shorebirds out on the seawall screaming a warning about life— her life! They seemed so real, but she couldn't be sure. She went inside, tore off a sheet of graph paper, opened a bag of Oreos and made coffee.

Math is hard, geometry is worse, she grumbled. It was past midnight. She was painfully tired. She would close her eyes for just a minute or two while the coffee was brewing. What happened next seemed so real. It was about Carmen.

Love is a rebellious bird
that nobody can tame,
and you call him quite in vain
if it suits him not to come.

Nothing helps, neither threat nor prayer.
One man talks well, the other's mum;
it's the other one that I prefer.
He's silent but I like his looks...

Love! Love! Love! Love!
Love is a gypsy's child,
it has never, ever, known a law;
love me not, then I love you;
if I love you, you'd best beware!

The bird you thought you had caught
beat its wings and flew away ...
love stays away, you wait and wait;
when least expected, there it is!

All around you, swift, so swift,
it comes, it goes, and then returns ...

you think you hold it fast, it flees
you think you're free, it holds you fast.
Love! Love! Love! Love!

Habanera from the opera "Carmen" by Georges Bizet (1875)

Miranda woke up face down on a piece of graph paper covered with black crumbs, disoriented and hungry. Apparently, the full package of cookies she ate last night wasn't enough— she was starving! It was 4 am. She had to pee like a racehorse, grabbed the coffee can, and thought about her strange dream...

While Harry may consider me a rebellious bird, the bird of the song, I am not out of control, not like a Gypsy's child, and certainly not screaming like a shorebird! Yes, I left him, and chose someone else. But I still love him! And I am done with Judas, done with the man who stole me away and ruined my life. Oh, if I could just have one more chance, I would never fly away again, I would always be true to you, Prince Harry.

A random thought, and then another. The palace priests always told Miranda to pray... that God could hear her. But she could not find the words, didn't know what to say, and decided that a holy God didn't want to hear from a sleepy girl who cheated on her husband. She would handle this herself. No one knew her situation or her heart better than she. Miranda took a sip of cold coffee and wondered, *does Harry miss me, too? Is it true in opera as in life? Does he know I think about him in the dark at night, tucked into the softest sheets from the bed we shared? Does he go to sleep alone and miss me, too?*

In the dark of the night, Miranda sighed. *From the depths of my soul, Prince Harry... rescue me, I'm waiting for you.*

Miranda woke to the sound of a construction crew banging around outside her boat. She was feeling sleepy and depressed after her strange dream. Ron had already emphasized the importance of getting the structures done so the boats could be shrink wrapped right away. A vaguely familiar voice shouted, "Wake up, Miranda! You're already behind schedule! Now, c'mon up here and show us what you've got... heh heh."

So this is what it's like to have three men as roommates. A toothbrush, washcloth, and a ball cap would be the most primping time would allow. Miranda zipped up her snow suit, grabbed her drawing and climbed up onto the dock. The men were already hard at work sawing and hammering, and not wearing their ridiculous ski masks. Apparently that little stunt was just for her.

The man making all the noise was Luke, the short man with the boat next door. Good looking but crude, Luke was a private pilot-for-hire who flew charters back and forth to Amman, Dubai, and Iraq... all over the Middle East. He's the one who couldn't wait to introduce Miranda to the infamous Captain Brad. Ron had already warned Miranda that Luke was a lady's man... said he had a beautiful but jealous girlfriend who kept him on a short leash. His boat was called *Sierra-Tango-Uniform-Delta*. Miranda thought for a moment and decided it suited him.

She reached into the pocket of her snow suit and pulled out a wrinkled piece of paper. Luke grabbed it, raised his eyebrows, and looked at her sideways. "You've done this before?" as if practically everyone had designed a superstructure for their aft deck.

"I did it last night. I was tired. It's not finished yet."

Ron was looking over Luke's shoulder. "Make a parts list. You'll need PVC pipes and joints, a hacksaw, some blades, and a good pair of work gloves."

Ron had a pick-up truck and was heading out to get replacement webbing and D-rings for a project he was working on. Miranda hurried down the steps into the galley where she kept her money, (not in the coffee can). That cash needed to last awhile, unless she wanted to invite Charlie back on board. She gave Ron the money up front. There would not be any favors on the dock this winter.

Her third neighbor, Greg, was the one with the dark brown eyes. Without his ski mask, he was strikingly handsome. Greg had the dock closest to the shore, before the ramp that led up to the marina building. He kept to himself more than the other two, and was certainly more refined, even bashful. Legend had it that Greg made his money as a day trader on the stock market. His sailboat, lines, cables, and canvas were in perfect order— all signs of a good neighbor. He affectionately called his Beneteau 40.7, "Bull Market."

Greg was taking a break for lunch and listening to Mozart's Don Giovanni (one of Harry's favorites) and there was a wonderful smell coming from the galley below. "I love to cook. Sometime you'll have to come over for dinner. I've adapted some very good recipes for the smaller galley, and I collect spices from all over the world. Do you like classical music? Anyway, just knock if you need anything." He had short dark hair, a perfect smile, and was wearing this season's best look from J.Crew— definitely not a pirate, but Miranda had been fooled before. She thanked him for the offer. When the storms hit, she would need all the help she could get.

"Plans fail for lack of counsel, but with many advisors they succeed." Proverbs 15:22

The dockmates told her it was a rite of passage for anyone who lived on the dock. Luke asked Miranda if she liked getting high, because that's what she'd have to do if she wanted to be part of "the team." He promised it would be an experience she'd never forget. The men snickered. Miranda ignored the comment and assumed it was just more college humor. She never smoked pot, never tried drugs, but loved alcohol and drank like a sailor most nights. Living just a few steps away from Jack's Steakhouse didn't help, where Gladys the bartender gave her drinks for free.

Drinking had ruined her marriage. She would have never cheated on Harry had it not been for the alcohol, and she swore it would not lead her astray again. Maybe cutting back to three nights a week would help. Miranda had never really dabbled in hard work beyond organizing her closet and colorizing her good t-shirts. But sawing through the heavy plastic pipe was way out of her league; it was grueling. By noon she had shed her snow suit and changed into a sweatshirt and jeans. The sun came out, she was sweating. In a way it felt good.

"Measure twice, cut once. Are you listening, Miranda?" Luke was getting on her nerves. He was bossy, a know-it-all... a pirate to be sure, but strangely appealing. One mistake and she was never going to hear the end of it. Miranda didn't realize how important it was to check every angle and follow the drawing exactly. It was hard to make a straight cut. *Sawing was hard, period!* Even so, when she started to put the pieces together her project began to take shape.

She stepped back to take a look. In her heart she was dancing like a wide receiver in the end zone, but gave herself a discreet pat on the back instead. Miranda took off her leather gloves. Her palms were red and blistered, and her nails were shot, but accomplishing something on her own, without Harry or anyone else telling her what to do, made Miranda feel optimistic. She put on her gloves and kept working.

It was getting cold and Miranda slipped back into her snow suit. She was gathering up leftover pieces of PVC, sweeping off her dock. Ron told her the shrink wrap was available in two colors, blue or white, but anyone who ever chose blue went clinically insane before the thaw. He suggested white and Miranda agreed.

The top of Ron's mast was 60' 1" from the waterline. He strapped her into the bosun's chair and made sure she was tightly secured. Now she knew what the webbing and D-rings were for. It had been a great day on the dock, a day of success and new friendships. The men pulled on the cables and the bosuns chair moved slowly up the mast. Miranda got high and she loved it up there! Winter was coming, the structures were ready. "Good job, Miranda... you're gonna make it," shouted her mates. "You're gonna make it!"

Seeking Miranda

Guard your Heart

In the parking lot, Harry watched Miranda from the seat of his new Porsche 911 GT3 (limited production, 0-60mph in 4.5 seconds). Miranda was no adventurer, that much he knew. *What is she doing up there? And isn't that the snow suit I bought her in Aspen? That mast has got to be filthy!* He fondly recalled that even when she skied she kept a red lipstick in her pocket for touch-ups. *And who are those rough-looking men cheering her on?*

Harry frowned. His ex-wife had a lot of explaining to do. Miranda was captivated by the view of the lighthouse, the cold embrace of Lake Michigan, and the quaint shops on Bridge Street below. But most of all, she loved the sight of her boat, her new symbol of guts and glory. It wasn't until Ron and Luke lowered her carefully to the ground that she looked toward the parking lot. Luke shouted, "Welcome to the team, Miranda... I can't believe you made it!"

There were toasts, high-fives, and congratulations all around as she watched Harry Stowe walk down the ramp, not looking pleased. Even so, he was more handsome than ever; tall and fit and wearing those gorgeous loafers he bought on their last trip to Italy. Miranda hadn't been shopping in ages (except for West Marine to order replacement parts). Come to think of it, she did not miss shopping at all. Harry smiled, hugged her, and kissed her cheek. But she could sense him scowling at her friends. He was always the jealous type and liked being in control. Even before she made the introductions, she could feel his anger starting to boil. She was still his ex-wife, after all, and he did not like what he was seeing. Miranda put her hand on Harry's arm and quietly guided him away.

"Love is patient, love is kind. It does not envy, it does not boast, it is not proud. It is not rude, it is not self-seeking, it is not easily angered, it keeps no record of wrongs." 1Corinthians 13:4-5

The spectacle of the tall PVC structures and the festive atmosphere on the dock took Harry by surprise, that's all. Following tradition, he asked permission to come aboard. Miranda did a quick mental inventory to determine whether there was anything down below that she didn't want him to see, like the coffee can, a fifth of scotch, or any signs of Charlie's visit Thursday night. She asked him to take off his shoes so they wouldn't mark the clean white deck. He scoffed, and came aboard.

Harry seemed surprised. Since he first saw the old boat, *Seeking Miranda* had been transformed into a warm, enchanting hideaway. The mahogany woodwork looked rich, even though it needed another coat of varnish. Her little cuddy cabin, the place where she slept and read and dreamed at night was as luxurious as their bed at home— almost. A fringed chenille throw covered the electric blanket that Charlie brought her the other night. Life was good.

Harry was taken aback by her lavish quarters and silently wondered where she got the money to do all this. Miranda was stunned that she really did not care what he thought. Was she finally growing up? Gaining a vision for herself as a capable adult instead of someone's arm candy? Harry eased into the reason for his visit. He cleared his throat, smoothed back his hair. He wanted Miranda to come home, back to the castle where she belonged. She opened her eyes wide, couldn't believe it. He said they could put the past behind them and start over. Harry still loved her. Miranda fought back tears. She never expected this. Dreamed about it, but never thought it could happen. Yet, she had an unexpected sense of trepidation.

"Above all else, guard your heart, for it is the wellspring of life." Proverbs 4:23

Harry drew close and reached over her shoulder. Miranda closed her eyes and waited for his kiss. How long had it been since she felt his lips against hers? She thought about those romantic mornings… how he kissed her goodbye while she lingered in bed a while longer. With her dockmates yelling and banging around at the crack of dawn, she felt homesick for her old life with Harry. Instead of an embrace, Harry reached for a CD on the shelf behind her. Dvorak Symphony No. 9 in E minor, Op. 95. Harry looked at the CD cover and noted that the Solti/Chicago Symphony recording was especially nice. When he pressed play, the dark, tentative phrasing that introduces the first movement swept through her soul and carried her back in time.

The Palace Theatre in Providence had been fully renovated, its domed ceiling painted in muted pastels and gold leaf. An imposing chandelier glowed then faded as the house lights darkened. Harry preferred the privacy of his box seats, but on that night, he chose to sit among the ordinary concert goers in the loge— an opening night celebration, indeed! It was the last time they saw Dvorak No. 9 performed together.

Of course, Miranda's gown was stunning— a maze of twisted black straps, a daring neckline, and a high slit to the top of her long, tan legs. It looked like the dress worn by actress Demi Moore in the film, *Indecent Proposal.* In the movie the gown is a gift from a handsome, controlling millionaire played by Robert Redford. He adorns her like a princess, makes her feel special, then offers her a million dollars for her companionship. In the movie, she says yes, and the aftermath leaves her bitter and broken. While she wasn't sure why, thinking about that movie always made Miranda feel bad.

Harry shuffled his feet, trying to get comfortable in the cozy dinette. They listened. The "Adagio-Allegro Molto" begins with a pensive melody that belies the fury just ahead. Without warning, an intense dialog erupts between the brass, string basses, and timpani, their dominant voices overpowering the gentler flute and oboe. The trombones boldly announce their presence; the French horns, fueled by their orchestral power and prestige carry on. They overestimate their importance, content to drown in their own noise.

A long crescendo ensues, beckoning the flute to reply. She must respond but she is timid. She plays a sweet silver song but doesn't know her own potential. She is the voice of a girl who is unsure, naïve, and full of wonder. The clarinet joins her for support, but the trombones scold her, demanding that she submit at once! She feels helpless, the horns are angry! But when there is silence, she quietly, beautifully sings... her courage a foreshadowing of a melody to come.

The flute maintains her position. She is a sparrow in flight, unburdened and happy! Harry listens to the music and sips his coffee. Then— dissonance in the French horns! Screaming, wailing like beasts! Their demands are cloaked in beautiful but misleading countermelodies that would seduce the unwary listener. The flute waits. Her song is clear... a flourish, light and free. She can't believe she is flying! The violins bring harmony and depth, the oboe adds his blessing. The brass chase her but she is already gone. Miranda lowers her eyes, thinks about the black dress, and remembers her view from the top of the world. She dries her tears and tells Harry she's not coming home.

"Above all else, guard your heart, for it is the wellspring of life." Proverbs 4:23

Brian Parker Hall

Harry was not Miranda's first husband. She was still in college when she met Brian Parker Hall. Working as a hostess part-time at Oliver's on the River was the perfect job. The steaks were delicious (and free if you worked there), the clientele was upscale, and the hostesses wore white, off-the-shoulder dresses that accentuated her narrow waist and deep tan.

One night, a man approached the hostess station and said, "Parker Hall, party of four." He was in town with a group of pediatricians who were attending a seminar at the University. Miranda was hard at work, paging guests and showing them to their tables. It was Friday night and the restaurant was slammed, with a forty minute wait.

She did not give him a second thought until one of the waitresses took her aside and said someone in the Parker Hall party wanted her to stop by their table. Brian was thirty-something, built like an athlete, with warm brown eyes and a nice voice. He introduced himself and asked if she would like to join him for a drink when she got off work. Miranda said she had plans with her boyfriend (which she did), but told him she was very flattered.

A month later there was another seminar and Brian-party-of-four and his colleagues were back at Oliver's. It was on that night, after Miranda was summoned to his table and politely declined again, that he told his friends he was going to marry the hostess who he hadn't even really met yet. On the way out the door he asked for her phone number. She smiled and reminded him that she had a boyfriend. He smiled back and said he understood.

Two weeks after that, he was back. He was alone this time and called the restaurant in advance to make sure Miranda would be there. Brian Parker Hall drove into town one last time to ask Miranda out on a date. He sat at the bar eating an appetizer and asked her to have a drink with him when she was done working. Brian was in luck. Miranda's boyfriend had just canceled their plans so he could get drunk with his college buddies. She was fuming and decided to accept.

Brian Parker Hall was drinking scotch. Even though Miranda was underage, she ordered one, too. It was the night her drinking career turned a corner, and not in a good way. But because Brian Parker Hall was a classy, successful guy, she wanted to seem sophisticated and make the right impression. It tasted like transmission fluid, or at least as she imagined it to be. Dr. Hall explained that as long as you drink top shelf liquor, you won't get a hangover and you wouldn't become an alcoholic. Miranda was relieved to hear that and ordered another.

They left Oliver's on the River and went to a club where a band was playing. The jazz was smooth, and by now, so was the scotch. Miranda liked talking to someone who was older and more intelligent. He was a pleasant change from her frat house beau and his pals. When he dropped her back at the restaurant, it started to rain. Brian Parker Hall walked her to the spot where her car was parked. They both got wet, and instead of grabbing her and kissing her, he hugged her goodnight. She thought she might like to see him again and gave him her number.

Miranda quickly lost interest in campus parties, and stopped spending all her free time with her boyfriend. His roommate's claim to fame was that he could jam the cable box with a pair of toenail clippers so they could watch the Playboy Channel for free. The others were somewhere further on down the food chain.

Brian Parker Hall drove back into town for their second date. Miranda lived in an old brick house off campus that had been converted into apartments. She lived on the third floor, an attic nicely furnished, with two rooms divided by bamboo hanging beads... very Sonny and Cher. A row of potted plants sat on a shelf by the window looking thirsty and sad. Miranda stashed her dirty laundry and put a stack of dirty dishes in the oven so the place would be presentable if Brian came up for a drink.

She was waiting by the door wearing a white sweater dress, three coats of mascara, tall black boots, and a wool coat with a Peter Pan collar— Elvira meets Jackie Kennedy. Brian pulled up in a late-model Ford LTD Country Squire, a family man ready for a family. A Frank Sinatra song was playing on the radio. It was one Miranda had heard before, and Brian began to hum along.

"Out of the tree of life, I just picked me a plum... You came along and everything started to hum... Still it's a real good bet, the best is yet to come." He looked at her and grinned. They had dinner at a fancy restaurant and exchanged stories of their hopes and dreams. Brian was an only child, his dad died when he was young. His mother raised him alone but could not give him all the material things the other kids at school took for granted.

After graduating from college then medical school, he was determined to meet and exceed the success of any of his classmates. Brian Parker Hall was ambitious. They toasted to nothing in particular, but the golden glow of the scotch predicted a celebration. Or was it a warning? This was more than just a new boyfriend, thought Miranda. This was a major lifestyle upgrade— *or could be.* Brian was thinking the same.

He dropped her back at her apartment, kissed her on the cheek, and hugged her goodnight. He didn't invite himself up, so neither did she. When he called the next day and invited her to his home for the weekend, Miranda was very excited. He was so smart, and kind, and such a gentleman— not the type of man a girl would have to worry about. And besides, she couldn't wait to see what the world of Brian Parker Hall looked like.

That week in English class she was doodling on her composition notebook, looking forward to her trip, and taking a secret glimpse at what her future might hold. In perfect cursive she practiced writing *Mrs. Miranda Parker Hall... Dr. and Mrs. Brian Parker Hall... Merry Christmas from Dr. and Mrs. Brian Parker Hall.* She continued to daydream and doodle all the possibilities, and wondered about Brian's plans for her very special weekend.

On the day of her trip the weather was especially bad. Miranda hadn't finished digging out her car from the latest winter storm, and now they were calling for *ten more inches!* She didn't tell anyone she was going— not her parents, her friends at school, and especially not the girls at work, although they suspected. No one even knew she was seeing Brian Parker Hall, so how could she explain leaving campus for a date that was 50 miles away?

Driving that far in the dark, all alone, during a blizzard was probably going to be dangerous— even Miranda could see that. But in her imaginary world, she had a vision of the perfect weekend, a perfect plan, and a future that fairy tales are made of. She hoped it would be more like Cinderella, less like Little Red Riding Hood. Even if the roads were passable, she didn't want to drive all that way and get eaten by the Big Bad Wolf.

From behind the wheel of Miranda's 1974 Super Beetle, the situation already looked bleak. She wasn't a great driver even in the best conditions, and had a few minor dents and dings to show for it. It was Friday night and traffic was heavy on Trowbridge Road. Sheets of freezing rain were beginning to ice up her windshield. According to the map, she would follow U.S. 27 to I-69 which she had easily done before. But once she got out on I-96 west to Providence, it was anybody's guess what might happen.

Miranda turned on her CB radio, the one her dad gave her when he upgraded to a more powerful unit last spring. When her family went on vacation every summer, he tried his best to learn the trucker's lingo, but never caught on. Miranda, on the other hand, loved the buzz of the radio with all the fast talk and crazy characters that kept the banter going. As she merged onto 96 West, the snow was coming down hard and it was getting dark outside.

A row of semi-trucks stayed in the right-hand lane, spraying waves of heavy slush onto the windshields of cars trying to get by. Traffic was crawling at 45mph and starting to slow. It was cold inside the car. The VW Beetle was never known for putting out good heat, and turning up the defrost only made things worse. Except for a maze of brake lights ahead, Miranda could not see a damn thing. Her fear of highway driving was catching up with her and she started to panic.

"Um... breaker one-nine, you got a radio check, c'mon?" It was one of the things her dad used to say.

"You got the Bald Eagle, little lady. You're comin' in loud and clear... what's your twenty?"

"Um... I'm on I-96 westbound about five miles past the split. I'm trying to get around these trucks but these jerks won't let me get by... and I can't see a damn thing... and I don't know if— "

"What kinda rig ya drivin' there, little lady... maybe I can give ya some pointers."

"It's a red VW Super Beetle with—"

"...with a big green Spartans sticker on the bumper? And a big crease where it looks like ya backed into a phone pole?"

Uh oh. Miranda was pretty sure she was talking to the same guy she just called a jerk. She was also pretty sure that he was in the cab of that big rig looking down at her.

"Okay, Lil' Red... Little Red Riding Hood... that's your handle now, so let's pay attention." Bald Eagle and his brother, Pork Chop, told Lil' Red to back off the hammer and wait for the two trucks to put some space in between them. Bald Eagle pulled ahead, Pork Chop flashed his lights, and Miranda eased safely into the right lane between them. In trucker language they call it the "rocking chair"... a protected place between two big rigs with trustworthy taillights to guide her. She could see the road again and followed Bald Eagle all the way to Providence. "We knew ya could do it, Lil' Red. Now let's talk about them two guys you was callin' a jerk...

By the time she made it to her exit, Miranda was exhausted, cold, and needed to find a lady's room. It had been a long and difficult journey. She was deeply grateful for the help of her trucker friends, who were not jerks after all. But she was afraid to go any further. Even with the plow trucks keeping the main roads open, the town of Providence, Michigan was completely snowed in. She stopped at a gas station and used the pay phone to call Brian. He told her to stay put, lock the doors, and wait for him to come get her.

When Miranda hung up and walked back to her car, she slipped on an icy patch and fell. Her new wool suit was split open in the back and soaked with gray slush and road salt. When she tried to stand up she saw that her hand was bleeding. She was too tired to cry and cried anyway. There was nothing Miranda could do but wait to be rescued. Finally, Brian came and scooped her up in his arms, pretended not to notice her wardrobe malfunction, then took her home. They could pick up her car in the morning.

He gave her a pair of his extra-large sweatpants and a T-shirt with the name of his alma mater. She took a hot bath and washed away the day's drama from her mascara-stained face. Brian canceled their dinner reservations and prepared his bachelor's special: Mrs. Paul's Fish Sticks, Tater Tots, and milk. Miranda was starving and didn't complain. They sat in his rustic family room by the fire, laughing about his cooking skills and her courageous drive, sipping scotch late into the night. She got drunk, blacked out, and woke up in the guest room the next morning, safe and warm. She could not wait to see what the day would bring.

Right away she could smell bacon frying. If Brian Parker Hall was trying to impress her, he was doing a really good job. Once dressed in a subtle but sexy warm outfit (Guess jeans, the same Enzo boots, and a flattering sweater), Brian warmed up the car and suggested they go for a ride. He took Miranda on a driving tour of the nicest places in town. New schools, a snowy white park, and shops on the square. There were restaurants dressed up for Christmas, a publishing company, and streetlamps with wreaths and red bows. Providence was very charming.

With pride and a grin, Brian drove her past his office— proper and traditional, a picture of success. Outside of town the sprawling countryside was covered with snow, but promised a sea of velvety grass in the spring. Miranda looked forward to it. He drove her through a neighborhood of grand old estate homes, a clubhouse with the walks already shoveled, and a sign marking the spot where the residents played croquet. He gestured and indicated that this is where the Brian Parker Hall family would live someday. A family man waiting for a family...

That night Brian got down on one knee and proposed. Miranda acted surprised, blushed, and said yes, watching as he slipped the diamond on her hand. Brian Parker Hall was not surprised by her answer, and neither was she.

Elizabeth Taylor

Miranda was not Elizabeth Taylor, that much she knew. Aside from hanging out with other average-looking girls and assorted misfits in high school, Miranda was not popular, had more bad hair days than anyone she knew, and had never been on a date. The more voluptuous girls wore push-up bras, clingy T-shirts, and stylish shoes to show off their legs. Miranda was flat chested and wore knee socks and dresses from Sears. The low self-esteem that spiraled from her lack of status as a girl would haunt her and affect her choices for years to come.

Her social skills were awkward and limited. Academically, however, Miranda excelled. She had a habit of sitting in the front row and correcting her less capable teachers when they made mistakes in class. She read books that were far too sophisticated and sexually graphic for her age. When she was called into the principal's office, she had no idea why. Her teachers were fuming; her classmates, not impressed. What Miranda considered a thoughtful contribution to the education of her peers, only compounded her woes.

To calm her anxiety, she kept an empty perfume bottle— Loves Baby Soft— filled with vodka in her locker, taking a sip before the school day began, and between classes as needed. Alcohol was a source of comfort. Though her parents were not drinkers, there was a shelf full of bottles left over from a holiday party hidden in the pantry. As long as she didn't get caught, it was hers for the taking.

School was a social life of one, and Miranda eventually accepted her place. She was lonely. Based on her track record as a chronic outcast, she knew the odds of being proposed to again and again throughout her lifetime were nil. Brian was it! He was "the one!" Miranda was not Elizabeth Taylor— of course she said *yes!* Brian Parker Hall was the perfect catch, not just for her, but for any girl who wanted to get married and live a happy life. Even though she hardly knew Brian, she would be a fool not to marry him.

Michigan State had a satellite campus just outside of Providence, and Miranda started classes soon after they got married. It was her junior year of college. She stopped sitting in the front row and answering all the questions. She bought trendy new clothes at The Limited and took extra time with her hair and make-up. And instead of a worn book bag, she carried this season's new Gucci tote, (monogram canvas, traditional blue and red cloth stripe). There was just enough room for her books, her American Express card, and a lipstick.

Miranda learned to be more outgoing with her classmates until it began to feel natural. Her efforts quickly paid off. She made friends and loved her new place in college life. But in spite of her transformation, sometimes she felt overwhelmed and sad for no reason. It was getting hard to maintain her social energy and academic high. She worried that her old lonely high school days would return. And that's when the depression set in.

The couple's family doctor recommended a reputable psychologist, a Christian counselor who was an appropriate choice since she and Brian were active in the church. He asked her lots of questions and gave her a handout with some things to read from the Bible. Miranda was a quick study. She memorized the verses and repeated them like a parrot perched on his fake leather sofa. It was only her third visit, and even though she didn't feel any better, he pronounced her cured. He was giving religion a bad name. It was a short relationship.

Miranda continued to get worse. There were many appointments with many doctors after that. There were doctors in the city and doctors in town, and one whose hourly rate was more than her husband's car payment. There was an expert in the use of psychiatric drugs, a hypnotist, and a man who smoked pot in his office before she arrived. She saw a young Korean doctor who spoke little English but was quick to prescribe the exact drug the expert had rejected. The side effects were horrible, and the pills were discontinued before any real harm was done.

One psychiatrist, at her first appointment, gestured toward three photos on his desk of his beautiful children and said he wished he had never become a parent. He seemed more depressed than she. Another doctor, a woman who was always beautifully dressed and wore expensive shoes, prescribed pills for depression, pills for anxiety, pills to sleep, and more pills to wake up. When Miranda asked whether there was any risk in taking so much medication, she replied that everyone has to die sometime.

The last doctor she saw was a renowned psychiatrist who lectured all over the world on the subject of bipolar disorder, which in those days was called Manic Depressive Illness. Armando Ramirez M.D. was a Freudian psychiatrist who trained at the famous Menninger Institute in Topeka, Kansas. Menninger was the premier school of higher learning for much of the twentieth century.

In the Freudian tradition, Dr. Ramirez loved to hear about Miranda's dreams, sexual fantasies, and childhood memories, drawing farfetched conclusions from every small detail. Miranda could tell he enjoyed his work. He administered the famous Rorschach inkblot test, and Miranda made every answer as amusing as possible— a naked lady riding a bull, a naked lady climbing the Statue of Liberty, a naked lady climbing a naked lady. Unfazed, he never even looked up from his notes.

Dr. Ramirez was worldly, confident, and spoke with a strong accent. A man in his sixties, he was strangely appealing. Miranda liked answering his questions and flirting with him, hoping to graduate from psychoanalysis as quickly as possible. She saw him twice a week for nearly a year. Her appointments were always in the morning.

Typically, there was no one else in the building during her hour. His staff occupied the first-floor business office and did not arrive till later. The private offices on the floor below were occupied by professionals in related fields, operating on their own schedules. Only his office occupied the third floor. So on those early mornings, instead of coming in through the lobby entrance, Miranda would follow Dr. Ramirez as he climbed up the rusty fire escape of the grand Victorian mansion to a steel door with no window. Always dressed in nice clothes and tall, suggestive shoes, she wondered if falling down and breaking a heel would be considered a Freudian slip. *Hilarious.*

When the door opened, the fire escape led into a vast space, dark, and beautifully furnished. It took a few minutes for her eyes to adjust before she could see the nineteenth century European antiques that lined the walls, some with elaborate carving and mirrors. The crown molding was heavy and imposing. There were shelves full of dusty textbooks and diagnostic manuals. Once, when the grandfather clock next to the sofa chimed, Dr. Ramirez saw that it was a few minutes off. He got up from his chair and said, *"one moment while I adjust my cock."* Another Freudian slip, or maybe he said it on purpose.

Professional journals with reviews of his research and articles he had written were stacked on a row of metal cabinets. Patient files, folders, and notebooks sat on his desk next to a colorful ceramic bowl, probably made by a child. No plants; no sunshine peaked through the heavy velvet drapes. The darkness made Miranda feel like she might suffocate. A red phone with a rotary dial sat on his desk and rang only when a person was being admitted to "Two-West," the psych ward at Providence General Hospital. Miranda considered whether she might be next, and just how crazy she had to be to qualify.

The office was a chamber of puzzles and parody, all arranged to bend and break the human psyche. It was not designed to make anyone feel at home, except Dr. Ramirez. While Miranda rambled on, answering his questions, he was out of sight with his notebook, but always watching. During those months at the office at the top of the stairs, Dr. Ramirez made some bold observations and gave Miranda some bad advice.

She was young and impressionable. She had grown to trust him and was willing to try anything that might make her feel better. He reminded her that he was her doctor, that he knew best. She did as he asked. The damage was immeasurable. She never told Brian. But once that door was opened, she could never go back, never be the girl he once knew. Dr. Ramirez never figured out what was wrong with her, and her illness grew worse.

During the months prior to the onset of her depression, Miranda was a busy and capable member of the Providence community. She chaired the entertainment committee for the annual Symphony Ball, played golf and tennis with the wives at the club, and published her first newsletter as President of the local Orchid Society.

She gardened, she volunteered, she took classes and did well in school. Brian found her level of energy astounding. She was affectionate, sexy, even teasing him when they went out to dinner, begging him to take her home and take her to bed. Brian was never more in love or more satisfied. Now he was desperate and confused, but his devotion never wavered.

Their home was warm, gracious, and beautifully decorated. Miranda went shopping till her heart's content. Actually, she went shopping a lot before she became ill, sometimes spending so much that even Brian, with all his money, raised an eyebrow at their credit card statement. But that was okay. He just wanted her to be happy. If buying pretty things would make her feel better, it was okay with him. He just wanted his wife back.

Mavis Jackson was a member of the First Street Baptist Church and a bartender at the club where the Parker Halls belonged. She had known poverty, heartache, and the trials of raising six kids on her own. Miranda was stopping for a drink more often than she should, sometimes sitting at the bar while her friends played nine holes, then lying to Brian about it. Alcohol no longer made her feel light and happy, the life of the party. Getting drunk only made things worse.

Try as he might, Brian could not help her. He was a social drinker and did not understand the direction that her addiction was taking. Miranda remembered their first date when he told her how people who drank expensive liquor would never become alcoholics or get hangovers. He was wrong on both counts. She blamed him for her drinking. And frankly, she was getting tired of all his questions.

Miranda liked talking to Mavis. She was understanding and didn't judge her. She had become Miranda's confidant and friend, making her laugh even on her worst days. And there was one other thing— she always said, *God bless you, and I am praying for you, girl...* There was something in her words that drew Miranda close, something she never felt at church on Sunday, something she couldn't quite explain. One day, whether by luck or by providence, Mavis told Miranda about a counselor at the community health center who had helped her with some of her own problems. Mavis reached across the bar, took Miranda by the hand, and made her swear she would call and get help.

Miranda kept her promise. Clinical Social Worker, Lydia Peyton-Pierce, was an attractive lady in her fifties. She was wearing this season's plaid navy and tan

Pendleton skirt, coordinating jacket, and a turtleneck that looked like cashmere. A big owl pendant swung on a silver chain around her neck. Miranda thought it looked ridiculous, but they were considered stylish in those days, so she decided to overlook it.

The only other piece of jewelry she had on was a big diamond ring, round cut, simple setting, with a plain gold wedding band. It was stunning, nicer than any diamond Miranda had ever seen. And it made her wonder, *What on earth was this lady doing at a clinic to help poor people? It's not like she needed the money...*

Lydia Peyton-Pierce listened to Miranda talk about her life, her profound and unexplainable sadness, and her lack of interest in the things she used to enjoy— like school, her orchids, her marriage. Miranda looked down at her hands and scratched at her badly neglected cuticles. She told Lydia about the good times she spent with Brian and the mood swings she experienced during their three years together.

At the end of their session, Lydia Peyton-Pierce leaned forward in her chair, looked into Miranda's desperate face and said, "I have good news. You have a condition called bipolar disorder. There's no cure, but there *is* a way to treat it! Why don't we work on this together? I think I can help you."

Lydia made an appointment for Miranda to see the clinic doctor for some tests, then set up a time to see her the following week. "Let's meet at my private office and save that seat for someone who really can't afford to pay, hmm?" Though dressed in Chanel for her appointment,

Miranda had fudged a few numbers on the clinic's patient questionnaire, making herself look poor enough to qualify, at least on paper. Now she had been caught in a lie. She wasn't going to pull anything over on Lydia, and she decided not to try. Lydia wrote the address of her office on a piece of paper and handed it to Miranda. *"I'm located downtown on the square, right next to Stowe Publishing."*

Seeking Miranda

The Diagnosis

Lithium carbonate is a salt that appears on the table of chemical elements. It is a widely used and studied medication for treating bipolar disorder. It helps reduce the severity and frequency of mania, and also helps relieve depression. More than 2 million Americans are affected by the disorder each year, with many more going untreated.

Miranda read all the material she could find about her new medication and soon she began to feel better. Lithium did not produce a noticeable effect, not a buzz or a high. Instead, it was the lack of any appreciable sensation that stood out the most. Her thoughts were not racing, she wasn't staying up all night, and the excesses that used to drive her had lost their control.

Waking up and taking a shower every day started to feel good again, as a balance in her moods returned.

Feeling "well" was unfamiliar, and participating in a life with less sparkle and fizz felt awkward. She noticed that the paintings she did in art class were no longer dark and dramatic, or conversely, screaming with zeal. Colors were not dripping from the canvas to inspire her. When she sat down to write in her journal the words were precise and mechanical. And where she used to doodle cute little drawings down the margins of her schoolwork, there were squiggles of one dimensional frustration where the pictures used to be. She told herself she would adjust.

Looking back, Miranda could see how bipolar disorder had impacted her life from the time she was a child. Of course at the time, she didn't know she was different. She recalled a trip to Walt Disney World with her family just before her tenth birthday. She was so excited about going on vacation, she could hardly sleep at night. Her parents decided to stop and see the sights at historic Saint Augustine, a town on the east coast of Florida discovered by Ponce de Leon a long time ago. Some men in a nearby town were not happy that the French were going to settle there. They called for a mutiny, became pirates, and attacked the Spanish ships. There was a lot of fighting after that.

Pirates were of no particular interest to Miranda in those days, but that would change with time. They had nothing to do with Mickey Mouse or Space Mountain. But on that day in Florida, something happened. The cannons, silent to the rest of the visitors, roared with rage inside her head, and the famous Fountain of Youth spit its historic venom all over her. On that day something drew Miranda away from a happy childhood and into a dark place her family knew nothing about. The historic landmark ridiculed her in all her despair. Her mother's insistence to pose for the camera only made it worse.

Miranda played with this childhood memory over a scotch straight up at the club. It was Mavis's day off and it was safe to have just one, not that she had anything to hide. Lost in stories of the past, she wondered if she had ever experienced what it was like to be "normal." Would the new, medicated Miranda ever feel at home with her new way of thinking, feeling, loving, spending? She was a tourist in a foreign land who had never studied the language.

In the years following the Florida trip, Miranda was afraid of getting swallowed up by those days of Saint Augustine all over again. At the time, parents didn't take their kids to see a doctor about mental illness. And those that did rarely came home with a bipolar diagnosis. Miranda was glad she didn't end up a child psychiatrist's guinea pig, sampling new drugs willy nilly. There would be time for that later, when doctors prescribed a veritable candy store of pills for her to choose from. She looked back and wondered how her younger self survived.

Miranda knew this was how it had to be. With Lydia Peyton-Pierce at her side, the support of her loving husband, and a bottle of Lithium, she was hopeful that she would fall into step and become like everyone else. But when Lydia asked again whether she had stopped drinking, Miranda couldn't lie. Although she cut back, she just couldn't give up alcohol.

Lydia told Miranda if she didn't stop drinking, the medication wouldn't work. Miranda felt like the lithium was working fine and that cutting back on her drinking would be good enough. Between her weekly sessions, Miranda gave this issue some serious thought. She set out to prove that her drinking was really not that bad, and that certain people— Brian, Lydia, Mavis— were just trying to control her. For one thing, Miranda never drank alone. She was either with Brian or at the club surrounded by quality people. You'd never find her hiding out in a bar someplace, trying to keep it a secret. Also, she never drank at home. If she was in the mood to have a drink, she and Brian always went someplace proper. There were no empty glasses on coasters in the Parker Hall household— Miranda had more class than that.

And what about all those times when she didn't drink for three or four days in a row? That is not the pattern of a real alcoholic. And except for some bad hangovers, there was little evidence that she was sick with an addiction, none whatsoever! If Miranda really had a drinking problem, surely by now she would have some symptoms: Weight loss? Tuberculosis? Throwing up blood? She had no signs of alcoholism— Miranda was doing just fine.

She knew what a real alcoholic looked like. She watched a documentary on PBS about some disruptive men who lived under a bridge and took turns sleeping in a cardboard box. They were dirty and drank cheap whiskey morning till night. Miranda never drank before lunch and she was always impeccably dressed, groomed, and accessorized. Obviously, these were signs of a *social drinker*, nothing more— and it was time for people to stop pestering her about it!

She honored her commitments and responsibilities that were part of her busy life in Providence. Had she ever shown up late for a board meeting? Or a symphony concert? Or missed a deadline for the Orchid Society newsletter? Or gotten a DUI? No, no, no and no! People could always count on Miranda, that much she knew!

Some of the women at the club were alcoholics, there was no mistaking it. They seemed lost and broken and looked like hell, sitting idly by the picture window overlooking the ninth green. They started drinking at noon, right there in the dining room for all to see. Miranda decided those tragic cases would be her secret measuring stick, her reverse role models. As long as they were in worse shape, she saw no reason to quit completely. She was in absolutely no danger by having a few drinks, *no danger at all!* Why couldn't everyone just believe her?

It was a beautiful day in Providence. Summer was winding down and Miranda was still trying to adjust to being normal. Brian was busy at the office doing sports physicals and Miranda was on her way to the campus for a final exam. She loved taking classes at her alma mater and Brian was delighted that she was moving in a healthy direction. Molecular Biology of Plants was the toughest class she had taken since graduating from Michigan State.

Since becoming active in the Providence Orchid Society, Miranda found that growing the rare, delicate plants had a calming effect and challenged her to study something new. She couldn't wait to tell the ladies about her thriving Slippers of Venus and a special fertilizer she learned about that stimulates root growth. She would write all about it in the newsletter.

Miranda was still drinking, but less than before. She was honest with her doctors, explaining that she was struggling with sobriety but was faithfully taking her medication. Lydia Peyton-Pierce recently told Miranda about her own struggles with alcohol, that she herself was an alcoholic. It was hard to believe that anyone as polished and smart as Lydia could have ever been drunk, much less a real alcoholic. But Lydia assured her it was so.

Miranda went to an AA meeting where Lydia was the first one at the long table to introduce herself. "Hi, I'm Lydia, and I'm an alcoholic." Miranda knew that Lydia hadn't been drunk since college, and if you counted her successful thirty-year career as a counselor, mother, teacher, writer, and volunteer, she was certainly much more than that. Miranda thought that was ridiculous, but listened to all the other ladies in the room do the same.

After the meeting, Lydia introduced her to some of the women and they all wrote their phone numbers on the back of a small, printed meeting schedule. She enjoyed listening to the speakers who talked about what life was like when they were drinking, what happened, and what life was like today, thanks to "the program" and their "Higher Power."

Some of the members had really struggled. A pretty girl named "Brittany" (close to Miranda's age) had gotten pregnant in her teens while she was drinking and using drugs. Her boyfriend was dealing cocaine out of his basement, and when she got caught with some of his drugs in her car, she couldn't talk her way out of it. Her dad was a judge in a neighboring county and things for Brittany could not have been worse. The situation became very public, her parents practically disowned her, and she had a miscarriage in the county jail.

That was her rock bottom. Today she is married to a wonderful husband, goes to college part time, and has two healthy children. She credits her sobriety to staying away from her old friends and the places she used to hang out, and attending AA meetings seven days a week. Like everyone else Miranda met at AA, she expressed her sincere gratitude to Alcoholics Anonymous, and "you people."

Miranda liked Brittany's story. It was inspiring and helped Miranda see that she needed to make some changes in her own life before she really screwed things up. But what about Brian's colleagues who liked to drink— his civic groups, professional affiliations, and the couples they golfed with at the club... not to mention the Kiwanians, Rotarians, and Noon Optimists? The Parker Halls were a very social couple.

And what about the ladies who do lunch, and her friends at school who like to party? Even certain members of the Orchid Society had a martini at lunch, *or two!* How in the world was Miranda supposed to change all that? Was she not supposed to have friends? She got invited to practically everything! How could she just say no? She decided the rooms of Alcoholics Anonymous were not for her. Maybe her Higher Power could help...

Miranda always arrived at the campus early. She liked to sit in the parking lot and review her notes one last time before a test. But on this day, something wasn't right. She felt distracted and her thoughts were whirling, spinning, speeding out of control. This was not the way she wanted to finish out the semester. Against her better judgment, Miranda took a small sip of Vodka— a *very small* sip— from the bottle she kept in her car. She had taken a Xanax after breakfast and it was starting to kick in.

Over the past year Miranda had seen so many doctors and filled so many prescriptions that she had a huge inventory of anxiety pills and assorted psych drugs at her disposal. She lost interest in the tricyclic antidepressants and SSRI's, but the Xanax and Ativan always seemed to help. This was the first time she combined pills with alcohol, and when she got out of her car she wondered if that might have been a mistake.

Miranda fell asleep at her desk halfway through the essay question. The teaching assistant walked her out of the classroom and a guidance counselor drove her home. She later told the professor about her bipolar diagnosis and he graciously agreed to schedule a make-up exam. He warned her not to do it again. Her classmates, however, were not as compassionate. They talked behind her back and called her a drunk, which in a way was true, but they didn't have to say so. Her status as one of the "smart kids" was reduced to "college burnout," a label she knew was far beneath her. She hoped this would not get back to any of the couple's friends, and said a quick prayer to her new Higher Power, whoever he was. She promised never to do it again if he would help her just this once.

The following weekend was Brian's high school class reunion. He was beautifully dressed, looking very handsome, and basking in his hard-earned success. Miranda was no longer the ugly duckling, the shy girl standing against the wall wishing she was Elizabeth Taylor. Instead, she was the pretty girl in the expensive dress leaning against the bar. She joined some of the other bored spouses in a few shots of whiskey, a couple margaritas, and wasn't sure what else because that's when Miranda passed out.

Brian was mortified while his classmates looked on. The alcohol poisoning lasted three days and Miranda thought she would die. On Monday morning she was still so sick, weak, and dehydrated that Brian sent one of his assistants to the house to look after her. Controlling her drinking wasn't going so well. Her husband was disappointed.

Lydia Peyton-Pierce still believed in Miranda. The trouble was, Miranda stopped believing in herself. As weeks went by, her manic episode melted into another state of depression. She began to have thoughts that were purely erroneous, feelings that were based on what her illness and the alcohol were telling her. The more her depression consumed her, the more distorted her thinking became.

Continuing her graduate studies at the university was out of the question. Her behavior during the final exam, the thought of her classmates watching her stagger out of the room— she couldn't bear it. Even though a lot of her college friends got drunk every weekend, Miranda couldn't see it any other way. She was very sad about her future. She thought about leaving school, leaving Brian, and leaving everything else. Knowing she could end her life whenever she felt like it brought her comfort.

Miranda didn't care about Brian's classmates, people she'd probably never see again. As for the ladies at the club and her friends at the Orchid Society, they certainly wouldn't want someone like her hanging around and giving them a bad name. She was too great a risk— it was hopeless.

She also believed that Brian's disappointment in her could never be repaired. Come to think of it, her marriage hadn't exactly been what she expected. She wanted real excitement, not afternoons at the pool with a bunch of snooty women and their Chanel bags. Miranda had faced the fact that life with Brian was getting dull, or at least that's what her depression was telling her. Even with all their trips and fancy dinners, she still wanted more. Maybe the depression was coloring her thoughts, but she doubted it. Or maybe the medication was helping her to finally see the truth! Yes, that had to be it!

Brian's desire to start a family had always made him so endearing. Now he brought it up constantly, ignoring the fact that lithium and pregnancy do not mix, and being an alcoholic mom wasn't such a great idea either. Maybe if they wouldn't have become engaged on their third date and gotten married a few months later they could have talked about having babies in advance! Miranda blamed Brian for his lack of foresight. He was older and more responsible— he should have known better.

Lydia advised her not to make any hasty decisions, that according to her most recent blood test, her medication was below the therapeutic level. If she was willing to take an antidepressant on a short-term basis, along with the lithium, her mood would probably lift. And if she continued to judge her marriage so harshly, she could make a decision that she might always regret. This was a time to exercise good judgment, Lydia told her emphatically. But Miranda was certain she deserved a better life— more attention, more romance, and a man who had more time to fuss over her... in and out of bed.

One night after dinner, Miranda and Brian were having one of their regular discussions about starting a family. Brian wanted four, Miranda wanted a little peace and quiet without having to explain herself for the umpteenth time. She told Brian about *her* needs, the things that were missing in *her* life, that would make her truly happy. Brian said, "You will never be satisfied with anything I could give you, Miranda. What you need is someone who has already built his career... already hit the big time, a rich handsome guy with lots of money who can give you whatever you want. You need a man like Harry Stowe." Six months after that night at the dinner table, Miranda and Harry were married.

Miranda and Harry

Miranda first met Harry Stowe shortly after she married Brian Parker Hall. As the new president and editor of the Orchid Society newsletter, it was her job to proofread, add some finishing touches, and deliver the final edit for printing, just as the editors had done for decades. When Harry's father founded Stowe Publishing, the Orchid Society was one of his first accounts. Even after the business grew and took on many national clients, the company's warm relationship with the Orchid Society continued. With each quarterly edition, Brian grew more proud of his young wife for accepting a role of such responsibility and status. It was good for her to have a project of her own, especially one that was held in high regard in the Providence community.

Miranda always looked forward to dropping off the newsletter and going over the details with Harry. He was successful, charming, and well liked around town.

And his British accent was very sexy. Even as a younger man, Harry made a fortune doing what he loved. But because he grew up in a world of privilege and was heir to his father's publishing thrown, Brian resented his success. Miranda called him Mr. Stowe. He was older and mysterious, something she could not quite explain. Even so, she loved doing research and writing about the beautiful plants, and judging by his excitement when she arrived, Harry loved them, too! *Orchids are among the most lovely and coveted flowers in all the world,* he once told her. She took it as a compliment.

For no specific reason she could recall, Miranda always spent extra time picking out a pretty suit and making sure her lipstick was perfect. It was okay if her skirt was a little short. It was Dior, after all, and she was still in her twenties. She just wanted to look nice— a fresh manicure, a new pair of shoes, a spritz of Chanel No. 5, and she was ready to go.

Harry looked forward to seeing Miranda and always found a reason to schedule a second or third meeting to go over the details. Once it was to clarify a quotation in an article, "Orchids and their Evolutionary Relationships." Another time he needed to confirm the spelling of Cypripedium Calceolus. Even though Harry had his own dictionary, he wanted to get it just right. Orchids are very complex.

While Miranda sat at a traffic light fussing with her hair, Harry was busy rubbing his new Porsche with a diaper to enhance the car's mirror finish. She always parked behind Harry's office. It was next door to the building where Lydia Peyton-Pierce saw her well-to-do clients. So far, Miranda had avoided running into her, but made arrangements with Harry to use the back door of the building just to avoid a lot of questions. Not that Harry and Miranda had anything to hide because they didn't— at least not yet.

She acted surprised when Harry invited her to join him for lunch at Red Lobster, one of the nicest restaurants in town. They rode together in his shiny red car; he said the police called it, "arrest me red." It was one of many fast rides she would enjoy in the years to come. When things began to go downhill between Miranda and Brian, Harry noticed her tired eyes and the sadness in her voice. He was a caring and attentive listener. She told him about her situation at home without mentioning her drinking problem or bipolar diagnosis. She finally had those situations pretty much under control, so what would be the point?

After her divorce from Brian Parker Hall was final, she told Harry she was looking forward to some time being alone, just being single. She wanted to get to know herself again; Lydia Peyton Pierce agreed. Harry patted her hand and invited her to go with him to see "The Phantom of the Opera." It was playing at the historic Pantages Theatre in Toronto, and he had tickets for Saturday night. They would take his jet and be home the next day. After that weekend Harry was a phantom no more.

Miranda never regretted going to Toronto, except for one thing— over dinner, he told her he was married.

She was stunned! How could she have possibly have not known? As Harry fumbled with his escargot, she considered her dilemma. Maybe she could have asked someone. Lydia Peyton-Pierce ran in the same circles as the Stowes, but for some reason, she never said a word. Of course, Miranda kept the affair a secret, and never got caught, but still... There were no telltale photos on Harry's credenza at work, and of course, no ring on his hand. Miranda always wondered why he seemed so elusive.

There were members of the Providence Orchid Society who had known Harry Stowe for years, and mutual friends who sat on the Symphony Board, as did he. And when Miranda looked at the country club's membership directory, did she miss something? Had the pages where Mr. and Mrs. Harry Stowe were pictured somehow disappeared or been stuck together? Yes, there were many excuses. Maybe Harry was going to leave his wife anyway, and none of this would be her fault at all. Maybe the union of Harry and Miranda was meant to be. Maybe they would be together forever!

Truth is, all she had to do was ask Mavis. Although she was an honorable woman and very discreet, Mavis knew everyone. Not only would she have told Miranda the truth about Harry, she would have also told her it was wrong to be involved with him, or any married man for that matter. Mavis loved Miranda, and that alone would have made it necessary for her to tell her the truth.

"Thou shalt not commit adultery." Exodus 20:14

Even in her deepest moments of denial, Miranda couldn't pretend she didn't already know that.

The first big storm of the season was about to hit northern Michigan! At the marina, Miranda's dockmates were furiously checking their dock lines and fenders, while she sat at her little dinette doing her best to plan. The man on the Weather Channel said they were calling for snow after midnight; a nor'easter was on its way.

The boat hit the dock with a thud and the spring line stretched tight, creaking hard against the wind. Miranda's coffee spilled in her lap, a burning reminder that she was on her boat in the cold alone, and not at Red Lobster with Harry. Summer's glistening paradise was preparing for a direct hit, and the boats at the Boat Basin were about to get buried. It was three days before Thanksgiving. The sooner she could get out of Charlevoix and onto a plane to Palm Beach, the warmer and happier she would be. Miranda was not going to spend the holiday weekend in this mess. The storm was on its way!

Someone on the dock was shouting her name and it sounded urgent. "Unless you want to freeze to death, Miranda, you better put on your red snowsuit and get your butt out here to do your share of the work." Luke was pleasant, as always. "Just because you made it to the top of the mast doesn't mean you get the day off or any special treatment. Nobody here cares that you're a *girl!*"

To herself she said, *blah, blah.* She tuned out Luke's big mouth, freshened her lipstick, and climbed out into the cold. "I'll bring my tools if you bring yours, you jerk!" She was definitely part of the team.

She rushed down the pier and found Greg lying face down on the dock by his sailboat, his arm reaching way underneath, cheeks bright red. Miranda hurried over to him, asked if he had tripped or fainted. He mumbled something under his breath, held out his free hand, and asked her to pass him the cutters.

Before she could figure out what on earth they were up to, he asked her for three cable ties, two long and one short... *and,* to lie down on the dock, reach under the planks, and grab hold of the yellow electrical cord in his hand. It was the closest she had ever gotten to Greg. He was so cute, and such a good cook. But this was not a date... *this was a robbery!* They were going to steal electricity from the empty docks and run the extra power to their own. *She was Greg's accomplice!*

Electricity is a complicated thing. On the one hand, the thick yellow cord carries 30/amps, 125 volts. On the other hand, there were things that drew a certain amount of power— like space heaters that were taking on added importance as the temperature quickly dropped. Ron walked over to check their progress then launched into a detailed technical explanation of how power works:

"The electrical charge which flows into your boat..."

(Greg asked for more cable ties...)_

"... an effective voltage of about 120 volts..."

(and now the pliers, oops, almost dropped them...)

"... and therefore, watts = volts x amps. It's simple, really. Miranda, this is important... are you listening?"

This was for Miranda's benefit and she nodded gratefully. But all she really cared about was being warm, not starving, and having good hair. If she could plug in her hot rollers without blowing a fuse before breakfast, even better. Greg assured her, "Don't think of it as stealing, Miranda. Think of it as survival." It was his fifth winter at the Boat Basin. "We're paying a lot of money to dock here, so don't give it another thought." She handed him the cutters and passed him three more cable ties.

"Thou shalt not steal." Exodus 20:15

Everyone else was doing it, but something didn't feel right. Miranda considered whether the Ten Commandments still applied today and decided that when it's really cold out, there's an exception to every rule— and this was it. What Miranda did not know, was that people were praying for her— Brother John, Brother James, and her friend Mavis. Sometimes prayer is the most you can do for a loved one who is headed the wrong way.

The Storm

It was getting dark. Miranda quickly plugged in the heavy yellow cord, now carefully attached beneath her dock and running the length of the pier. They finished their project just in time. She wondered if the boaters who rent that slip in the summer would get a bill for her unauthorized winter use. She wanted to do the right thing, to act like a moral person, someone who Harry would be proud of. But she was busy getting ready for the storm, and there was no time to think about that now.

It was starting to flurry and the water was black as ink. The boat she called *Seeking Miranda* seemed smaller and more fragile than the day before as she watched the storm roll in. Miranda bundled up in all her heavy gear before making one last trip up to the lady's room and to see who was around in case she needed help. The flurries quickly turned to snow. Even her powerful floodlight could not cut through all her fear.

Speaking of Charlie, why was he never around when she really needed him?

Miranda always acted like she was bulletproof, fearless, and one of the guys. But really, that was all just for show. Not much had changed since her high school days when she wanted to fit in but never felt like she measured up. Getting drunk worked fine back then, but tonight getting drunk might get her killed! She had to stay sober for just one night, and have enough common sense to put her safety ahead of everything else.

Water crashed against the seawall; sprayed her face hard. She squinted against the wind and could feel the dock getting slippery beneath her feet. Her dockmates told her to put on ice cleats, stay low, and put down her swim ladder. If one of them fell in it would be the only way out of the water. Miranda knew hypothermia would strike within minutes.

In the dark waters she would never find her way out, drunk or sober. But there was no turning back now and she secretly wished someone would rescue her. She wanted Harry, Charlie, or even Brian to take her someplace warm and dry, to sleep in someone's arms again. Miranda missed being a princess and wondered how in the world things turned out this way.

There was a fat man standing against the wall beside the door to the lady's room. Miranda had seen him there before. He was a chain smoker, wrapped in a heavy down coat that barely zipped across his considerable girth. A trapper's hat was pulled down low over his eyes, and a runny nose was starting to freeze in his beard. He was gross and gave Miranda the creeps. She figured he was a maintenance man or a drunk who stumbled down from Jack's Steakhouse. Whatever the case, at this hour no one should be here. She thought about the shotgun she slept with at night. It gave her peace.

Miranda was heading back to her boat, bracing herself against the wind as the snow stung her cheeks. Greg's voice sounded distant. He shouted at her, "Miranda. Stay low. Go back to your boat. Grab a blanket and stay on the floor. Sleep in your snowsuit, put on a life vest. The storm will be worse than we thought. Now go! *GO*!" She looked back at the stranger, watching for the red glow of his cigarette, but he was gone. In an ominous voice, the wind howled.

"Be still and know that I am God." Psalm 46:10

She would take her Bible out of the Ziploc bag tonight. She thought she might need it.

The storm was raging now, the beast was poised to strike. Miranda scurried onto her boat, slipped on a step, and fell onto the aft deck. She was unnerved by the fear in Greg's voice. If he was so intimidated even with all his experience, where did that leave a rookie like her? She grabbed a handrail, pulled herself onto her feet, and sealed the little door in the shrinkwrap that was flapping in the wind. Out of breath, she made it down the steps to the cabin, which was toasty warm, thanks to the extra power from the dock down the way. She was grateful to be safe and out of the weather.

Miranda felt her stomach churn as the boat started to rock. She would not be having a snack tonight, probably not reading her Bible either. A blanket, her pillow, and a bottle of Pepto Bismol would have to do. Then another assault— a crashing wave, some cans of soup, a bottle of pills, and a cordless screwdriver fell hard at her feet.

The old boat was supposed to be watertight. But tonight, Miranda wondered if boat-builder George Garcia was thinking about a Lake Michigan snowstorm when he created the first aluminum Marinette three decades ago. She wondered if welded marine grade aluminum was strong enough to take what the night had to offer.

Miranda listened intently, waiting for the sound of the bilge pumps. *Oh my gosh— were they even working!?* With an ear to the floor, she became obsessed with the thought of her boat filling with water and her dockmates finding her lifeless body in the morning. She had to think fast before she submerged herself in thoughts of doom. Miranda reached up to the counter, fished around for a pencil, and grabbed a small flashlight. Then, crawling on her belly to the hatch in the floor, she grabbed the pull ring and heaved open the heavy panel. The bilge was dark, and vast. In the hollow space the sounds of the storm echoed.

Before she lost her nerve, Miranda put the flashlight between her teeth, took the pencil, and reached deep into the murky hull. She held her breath as she tripped the bilge pump with the eraser end of the pencil, hoping not to be electrocuted. A whirring sound told her the pump was working, and the lack of rushing water meant the bilge was dry. Thank God. Relieved, Miranda closed the hatch and wiggled back to her spot on the floor.

Just as she was patting herself on the back, the boat began to list and she puked all over her new Oriental rug, another gift from Charlie. He always came bearing gifts, and cash, and a smile. But none of that mattered tonight, did it... BECAUSE HE WASN'T THERE! And even if he was busy at work, he could have called!

This was the last straw. If it were not for Charlie, she and Harry would still be together. Miranda would forever regret looking into the eyes of the pirate who took what wasn't his. Instead of lying face down seasick in her own vomit, she would be at home taking a bubble bath while Harry smiled and looked on.

There in the storm, Miranda decided to end it with Charlie for good. She had enough money socked away that she didn't need him anymore. The area rug cost more than her first car— she hoped the dry cleaner made house calls. Soon she would be on a plane to West Palm Beach where she could relax and forget for a while. There was nothing to be gained by celebrating Thanksgiving alone in the snow. Somehow between the waves, and by the grace of a God she didn't even know was watching. Miranda drifted safely to sleep.

It was morning. Miranda popped her head out of the little zippered door. Blinded by a welcome sunrise, she was delighted by what she saw. What was once a dark howling wilderness was now a playground of giant white peaks and powder! Drifting snow stretched across the Boat Basin and covered the summer cottages nearby. If not for the fear of disappearing or getting stuck, Miranda would have run off the end of the pier and fallen onto her back to make snow angels.

All things bright and beautiful
All creatures great and small
All things wise and wonderful
The Lord God made them all.
Lyrics by Cecil Frances Alexander

It would have been a perfect day to ride the bosun's chair to the top of the mast and see the snow from way up there! The view of Bridge Street to one side (now crawling with snowplows), and Lake Charlevoix to the other would have been enchanting! Maybe Charlie was right— maybe she should have named her boat "Snow Angel" after all!

Still in her boots and the crusty, red snowsuit she slept in, Miranda stepped out of the shrinkwrap and couldn't believe what she saw. Her dock and the pier leading up to the boathouse were shoveled?! All the way up to the marina building... to the lady's room, too? Boat Basin management wasn't exactly big on customer service this time of year, and she was very happy that she wasn't going to have to do all that work herself. She didn't notice the man disappearing around the corner and into the parking lot.

Miranda headed up the ramp to the lady's room in a hurry. Staying sober last night was the right choice. It felt good to wake up clear-headed and not hungover. Other than being seasick and getting vomit all over the place, she felt fine! Maybe it was time to take another shot at sobriety. When she passed the Beneteau, she yelled at Greg to wake up and look outside. He was usually an early riser and Miranda knocked hard on his bow.

That's when she saw the note taped inside his sealed shrinkwrap door. *Miranda— Had to visit a friend last night who ran into some trouble during the storm. Back on the boat next week. Have a Happy Thanksgiving... Greg.*

Are you kidding me? He LEFT? After dishing out all that advice? Maybe he has a girlfriend— or boyfriend— he stayed with. Or maybe he couldn't stand to be out in the weather, all alone— like a girl! She would give him a hard time as soon as the group reconvened on the dock next Tuesday.

Miranda was the only one who toughed it out last night. She was either a hero or an idiot. Either way, it will be a great story someday. Just then, she spotted footprints much bigger than her own outside the lady's room. And cigarette butts near the door. What was that weird guy doing here this early? She wondered whether he hung around all night, which made absolutely no sense considering the terrible conditions. His presence at the Boat Basin disturbed Miranda a great deal, and she made a mental note to talk to some of the locals, find out who he was, and get to the bottom of this.

She looked in the mirror and noticed dark circles under her eyes. She needed to get more sleep. She brushed her teeth twice and took an extra-long shower. She could not wait to head up to Jack's Steakhouse for some breakfast, then make her way to the travel agency, just one block away. Her tickets to West Palm Beach would be waiting.

Miranda looked out into the parking lot hoping to catch the intruder causing trouble. But instead, she saw only one car, her own— brushed off, free of snow, windshield scraped clean. And the space around her car was shoveled, too?! Whoever was responsible did everything but start the engine and put a travel mug of hot coffee in the cup holder! She wondered about the mysterious man. People always surprised her.

Seeking Miranda

Palm Beach

Miranda was awake all night, too excited to sleep and eager for her vacation to begin. The first leg of her journey was a 39-minute flight from Traverse City to Detroit. She left the Charlevoix Boat Basin at dawn, eager to be out of the cold for a while. It was a beautiful day, the roads were dry, and freshly plowed snow bordered the highway. At Cherry Capital Airport, she followed the signs for long-term parking, checked her bag, tipped the porter, and passed through security. She arrived on time at Detroit Metro where she would board a non-stop flight to Palm Beach International Airport. She was spending Thanksgiving in the promised land.

Miranda stepped off the jetway and headed toward her gate until she found a set of monitors. Her flight was on time. There was a bar up ahead. A tacky neon martini glass with a big neon olive indicated the pub was already open for business. She had plenty of time, but couldn't risk getting drunk and missing her flight. Lately it felt like something wasn't quite right. She was restless and agitated; a top that wouldn't stop spinning.

Miranda was craving relief. She glanced again at the bar, men in suits heading in for a quick one. She was probably just tense from life on the dock— the blizzard, late nights, the mysterious chain smoker whose identity was still unknown. Miranda decided that all she needed was some rest, and that's exactly what she would do once she got to her hotel. The airport bar was calling. She would have one drink on the plane, then figure out the rest when she got there. She felt good about her plan.

Almost to her gate, she spotted a wall of beautiful glossy fashion magazines, the ones she stopped reading when she moved aboard her boat. While there wasn't much need for couture on the dock, she would definitely be doing some shopping in Palm Beach. Miranda looked at her watch, ducked into the crowded newsstand, and grabbed a Vogue and Marie Claire. She held them close and smiled— they had that new magazine smell! She paid the man at the counter, put away her wallet, and decided to have one drink.

She spun around to leave the shop still fumbling with the old Gucci Boston bag from Harry. The green and red canvas stripe showed a few signs of wear, but it was perfect for schlepping around the airport. The crowd shifted, inching their way closer to the counter, and Miranda bumped into the person in line behind her. She looked up, saw his face, and couldn't believe it. Silver hair, a ponytail, blue eyes— *It was the man in the navy blue blazer!!* He looked even more handsome than the night she saw him across the bar at Tommy's Gotcha, the night before she left Traverse City for good. But now, instead of a rocks glass, he was holding a thick stack of newspapers, with the Wall Street Journal on top.

He was soft-spoken and polite, and said *pardon me* as if it were his fault. Pressed up against him, she was at a loss for words. Her cheeks turned red and she could feel herself beginning to sweat under the weight of her Michigan State T-shirt, hoodie, and favorite jeans. *It was a bad moment to be dressed like a guy who lives on a boat in the winter.* Fortunately, Miranda was having a good hair day, and her Nars Jungle Red lipstick was perfectly applied. She met his glance, tried to smile. The man in the navy blue blazer touched her arm and said, "Hello, Miranda." She blinked hard, looked at her watch, hurried through the crowd and out of his sight. One mysterious stranger in her life was enough.

Her old cowboy boots went click-click-clicking past the shoeshine man, the Martini bar, and a frozen yogurt kiosk. She arrived at her gate with minutes to spare, and lingered out in the concourse, certain he was watching. Miranda resisted the urge to look back— *don't do it, don't do it!* Then she looked back anyway. The man in the navy blue blazer was standing outside the magazine stand with a serious expression. He was watching her. There was something about him she liked.

"A wise man suspects danger and cautiously avoids evil, but the fool bears himself insolently and is presumptuously confident." Proverbs 14:16

Miranda boarded the plane, fastened her seatbelt, and drifted off...

They taxied down the runway
"flight attendants take your seats,"
this plane will reach an altitude of 40,000 feet.
Miranda's sipping Vodka
soon her wings will touch the sky,
Ready to shop— it's time to buy!

Armani, Valentino,
fashion icons to embrace,
Chopard has diamond watches
that put on a happy face.
And sandals stratospheric
stole her heart at Jimmi Choo,
Only the best— Worth Avenue!

Chanel at Neiman Marcus
and at Saks Fifth Avenue,
A David Yurman bracelet
so expensive she bought two.
Her credit card was bleeding
though she wasn't halfway through,
Let's have a drink— at old Taboo!

The Donald and George W.
are seated near the bar,
Rush Limbaugh sat with Tiger Woods
and smoked a fat cigar.

She saw the ghost of Elvis
John Travolta, and Stallone,
Where's Giuliani?— *he just went home!*

Miranda's fully energized
a soaring manic high,
she smooths her hair and takes a breath
a long bipolar sigh,
The players on the bar stools
a performance they will see,
One more drink— will set her free!

But once it's set in motion
a torrential drunken binge,
a painful taste of ecstasy
a game no one can win.
No dignity, no self-respect
Miranda's lost at sea,
a bobbing cork— a memory.

Her fantasy vacation
wasn't all that she had planned,
she stayed out late, got wasted,
bought a swimsuit, got a tan.
She worried that misfortune
someday soon would come her way,
God to Miranda: *"It's time to pray."*

What happened next Miranda could not see coming. The scope of this disaster would change the course of her life forever. But sometimes even the worst circumstances can turn out to be a blessing. God had his eye on her even then...

Miranda's thoughts were losing altitude before her plane touched down in Traverse City. She thought about all the money she spent, the expensive clothes, the drunken nights, and an angry phone call with Charlie Fine. On the road back to Charlevoix an old familiar melancholy began to set in. Staring out at the northern Michigan countryside, she imagined the worst. At least she had the money to cover most of the wreckage.

There was probably a bottle of lithium somewhere on her boat. It had been several weeks since she'd taken any— she would get back on it tonight. Miranda made it to Charlevoix and stopped at the post office to pick up her mail. The clerk at the counter smiled, asked about her trip. Miranda gave a brief account. Her enthusiasm for life on the dock had waned since the storm, and now she just wanted to make it through the winter. An episode of bipolar depression could make that impossible.

She briefly looked through the newspapers, also a notice for an overdue library book, a credit card statement, an expired sale flyer from West Marine, and a Victoria's Secret catalog. She noticed a postcard from *Focus on the Family,* a religious group. *How that landed in my mailbox I'll never know*, she thought, as she nodded goodbye to the clerk.

Once in her car, she grumbled about the cold, started the engine, and sat in the parking lot looking at last week's headlines. On the front page of Sunday's society section there was a photograph of a lady, early fifties, with a shy smile. She wore a velvet dress, black with a portrait collar, and a delicate diamond necklace. Her auburn hair was in a loose up-do, her eyes were shining. She was very pretty. The man beside her wore a tuxedo and had a scar below one eye. His wild red hair was neatly combed. The man in the picture was her husband— it was Charlie Fine!! The caption beneath the photo read, *"Annual charity ball brings in record donations to aid city's homeless. Pictured are Marianne and Charlie Fine, event co-chairmen."*

Miranda stared at the picture. She squeezed her eyes shut wishing it would go away. She broke it off with Charlie when he called her at the hotel last night. Some ugly words were exchanged— it was really over this time. But that brought little comfort now. Miranda looked at the picture of Charlie's wife. *His wife.* She felt a wave of nausea and a churning in her gut. A migraine was gaining momentum. Marianne Fine looked so happy, and for that matter, so did he— no drink in his hand, no pinky ring, no signs of piracy whatsoever. On the night of the storm Charlie and his wife were together raising money for families in need. Miranda's arms were too heavy to drive. No wonder they called him Judas.

She pulled into the parking lot at Jack's Steakhouse. She needed to collect herself and ordered a double. Looking out over the frozen Boat Basin, she spotted two police officers, one next to Ron's boat making notes on a clipboard, the other walking up and down the docks. She watched as Greg and Luke joined Ron and the officers.

Miranda ran out of the bar, left without paying. She took the stairs down to the marina two at a time, still wearing her new sparkle flip-flops, her feet ice cold. She could see her breath, the frigid air burning her lungs with new intensity. She was glad it hurt. She had a bad feeling. Maybe the cops finally picked up the mysterious chain smoker for hanging out on the dock. It was about time somebody caught that guy. Miranda ran down the ramp toward her friends and specifically recalled locking the door to the cabin of her boat before she left. Maybe everything would be okay.

"For I am the Lord your God who takes hold of your right hand and say to you, Do not fear; I will help you." Isaiah 41:13

Miranda crossed the pier, approached her boat, and looked inside the shrinkwrap. The cabin door, with all its coats of varnish, was kicked in, broken, and splintered. It was a terrible sight and she knew it was about to get worse. She stepped down into the cabin. Despite the chaos of cushions overturned and her things strewn all about, she felt calm, sullen... a ship on a quiet sea.

Miranda was getting what she deserved— the whole thing with Charlie, for cheating on Harry, and for ending her marriage to Brian Parker Hall in such a terrible way.

Miranda picked up a fifth of scotch and took a drink. It burned in her throat. She took another, squinted her eyes shut, and swallowed hard. She might have wondered how this could have happened, but she was past that, deep into a place of resignation and doom.

Miranda took a deep breath, exhaled, and dropped down, down, down. Though still afloat, still aware of her surroundings, she clung to the blue swirl marble, sensed herself falling further, waiting for Charlie's good luck charm to drag her into the abyss. ... holding on, giving in, letting it go. The marble was gone forever; she fought back tears. She should call someone, perhaps, while she was still able. She couldn't remember Harry's phone number. More alcohol, another long drink from the bottle... not like a socialite sipping martinis on Worth Avenue, but a drunk under a bridge, the girl she swore she would never be. The officers said they'd be in touch and left.

She drifted, fell to a darker place... turquoise to Sapphire to midnight. She took a breath, exhaled through her nose, and watched the imaginary bubbles come out and rise to the surface. She shuddered, took a Xanax. It would help her relax on the way down... she took another. Miranda remembered Harry's number and dialed it. A girl answered. She decided it was the cleaning lady and hung up. Miranda thought she was so clever, thought an empty box of Tampax was a great hiding place for her money, that a burglar would never look there. She exhaled... more bubbles. Surrendering to the depths was beginning to bring some relief.

Tomorrow she would wake up and remember that all her money was gone, that she was broke. There was no one to bail her out this time; she had burned every bridge. While Miranda drifted briefly in that silent place, she took another drink, looked around at her boat. The adventure proved nothing; the joke was on her. She peered into the darkness, drank, and watched herself drift to the bottom. The weight of the water pushed against her with such passion and purpose, she thought she might like to stay. Sinking was painless, the depths were quite beautiful.

The bottle was empty, she was numb to the taste. *Take a breath, hold it...* the sound of her heartbeat was somber and dim. *Blow Miranda, blow! You must empty your lungs to go all the way down!* On the bottom there were stars, a flickering light... but no one else could see them. The colors embraced her, the marble was calling. She reached for it. Her long descent was complete... her heartbeat slowed and faded. It was her sea of tranquility, a dark lullaby.

Rock Bottom

Miranda stayed in bed. First for a day, then a week—maybe longer. She couldn't be sure. Her dockmates were sympathetic, bringing her mail, newspapers, and some groceries. She watched TV, did some reading, hardly ate at all. When she surfaced briefly from her hiding place, she was met with worried faces. Her skin was pale and dark circles hung beneath her eyes. She was so thin that even her red snowsuit could not disguise her frail figure.

The men had been robbed, too. An old Loran-C navigation system was taken from Ron's boat, Luke's TV and stereo were gone, and $100 in cash was stolen from Greg's Beneteau. He joked that his collection of spices from around the world was worth more than that. But they were all worried about her. Luke urged her to put on some red lipstick... said it would be like the old days of building superstructures and riding the mast. But

Miranda found little solace in their good-natured kidding.

Later that week, Ron brought news from the Detective Bureau. They completed their investigation and came up with nothing. The perpetrator had been there and gone. "Nothing? What about the guy from the lady's room?" Miranda demanded to know.

Ron shook his head, looked at her sympathetically. He knew she had it in for the guy. "He checks out, Miranda. His name is Neil Lipman. He spent Thanksgiving with his sister down in Traverse City. His brother-in-law is Joe Ramono, the big shot trial lawyer. He confirmed Lipman's story. He's not a suspect."

"Do they know that for sure, Ron? Couldn't he have driven up here late at night and ransacked the place? It's only an hour drive. If he wasn't hanging around waiting for his chance to rob us, why was he here at all?" Miranda rubbed her temples, put on dark glasses. The daylight was giving her a headache.

"Lipman was with Ramono all weekend. The night of the robbery they were at Tommy's Gotcha having a couple of beers. Joe is an expert DUI lawyer... sits at the bar and waits for his phone to ring. I'm surprised you don't know him." Miranda scowled. "I didn't mean it like that. Why don't you get a shower and come down to Greg's boat. We'll have some lunch."

Now that she thought about it, she did know Joe Ramono. She had a drink with him and a cowboy named Vince the night before she left Traverse City. It was the night she first saw the man in the navy blue blazer, the same man she ran into at the airport last week. Not that she cared, but she wondered again if he was married. And how did he find out her name?

Miranda knew Ramono was an honorable man, the perfect alibi. But that still didn't explain Lipman's presence at the Boat Basin. She wasn't about to let this rest, but for now she decided to take a long shower, brush her teeth, and put on some clean clothes before lunch. It was nice of Ron to invite her. She wondered what her dockmates were up to.

It was a crisp, sunny day on the dock. Greg had prepared a fresh shrimp salad, seasoned with horseradish and a tasty coral dressing. Homemade basil tomato bisque was served on Haviland china— fattening but delicious. He was a culinary genius and a wonderful host. How he keeps his priceless dishes from breaking in rough seas Miranda will never know.

Everyone was being really nice to her, glad to see her up and about— even Luke with his big mouth. There had to be a catch. Ron put down his fork and cleared his throat, the first to speak. "Miranda, we know you've been through a very tough time. We all feel just terrible about what happened. A robbery was the last thing any of us expected."

"You've done such a great job out here on the dock this winter," said Greg in a calming tone. "None of us thought you would make it, but you proved us wrong. You should be very proud for toughing out that storm. I left because I was seasick. I should have told you. But for now, we're starting to worry about you." They ate for a while in silence.

"Now there are a couple of things, Miranda. You need to quit moping around, stop drinking, and get your shit together. And... get a job! Yes, Miranda... a J-O-B job!" It was Luke. "Okay... so all your money was stolen and you have a raging hangover. But that's over now. No one is going to bail you out. If you can build an aft superstructure like a pro, you can certainly go out and get a damn job. It won't kill you to get up early and go to work like the rest of us. Any questions?"

Ron cleared his throat, indicating that Luke's turn to speak was over. "You're a smart girl. And a hard worker. Go to the library, ask for Jo. She'll help you get your resume in order." Miranda never saw this coming— an intervention over biscotti and espresso.

"The unemployment office is at Byrne and Second Street in Petoskey. I know this isn't your style, but it's a good place to start," She appreciated his kindness.

"And as for our late nights up at Jack's Steakhouse, those days are gone." Luke slammed his little espresso cup on Greg's linen placemat, spilling coffee that would leave a stain. You drink too damn much. You've got to start taking care of yourself or you're not gonna make it till spring!"

"We can't do this for you Miranda, but you know we're here," said Greg. "Would you like some tomato bisque to take back to your boat?" They all smiled; she was ravenous. "So you'll at least give it a try?" Miranda nodded her head, not sure she meant it.

"For this command is a lamp, this teaching is a light, and correction and instruction are the way to life." Proverbs 6:2

Monday morning. It was the first week in January and the lobby of the unemployment office smelled like wet parkas and cigarettes. Dozens of people, young and old, stood in line waiting for their number to be called. Maybe everyone was thinking the same thing— a new year, a fresh start. It was the last place Miranda expected to find herself, but with her money gone, she needed a job. She didn't know a soul in Petoskey, Michigan and wondered how much that might hurt her chances. She had been sober for two weeks. If she didn't stop drinking for good, she knew she would fail.

There were forms to fill out and applications to complete. And then she waited. With her resume in hand, she patiently shuffled with the crowd, inching her way toward an uncertain future. Harry would die if he saw her like this, an unemployed drunk, a princess no more. A lady stepped out from behind a closed door. She walked right up to Miranda and said in a pleasant voice, "My name is Janet, you can come with me."

Janet led the way to a cubicle at the end of a long hall. She was a black lady well into her sixties with a round face and a cameo pin on her blouse. On her metal desk sat a Poinsettia left over from Christmas, a small stone cross, and an "IN" box crowded with applications— not a good sign.

Miranda pulled nervously at the hem of her Dior skirt, tastefully paired with a cashmere sweater and her good pearls. Harry always said you should never outdress your interviewer. If her clothes did not give her away, the Manolos and Fendi bag surely would. Miranda pulled at her skirt again, worried that she had already made the wrong impression. Her self-esteem hadn't improved one iota since the seventh grade.

Janet's warm smile and curly gray hair gave her a motherly appearance that put Miranda at ease. She still wasn't sure why she was chosen to jump to the head the line when other job seekers were there first. Janet gestured for her to sit down. She took the completed applications, laid them on her desk, and asked Miranda what she was looking for.

Broken and defeated, she would have taken any job at all. She told Janet about living on her boat in the snow, stealing electricity, being robbed, missing Harry, spending too much money in Palm Beach, and her troubles with a pirate named Charlie. Maybe that was too much information to share at a job interview. But if Miranda had good judgment, she wouldn't be at the unemployment office in the first place.

Janet listened, nodded, and studied Miranda's resume. She took a business card from a plastic holder on her desk, and on the back she wrote an address. Janet stood up indicating their meeting was over and said, "Go talk to this man and do your very best. A proper suit would be appropriate." And as Miranda began to walk away, Janet said in a soft voice, "I'll be praying for you."

Seeking Miranda

The Resume

Monday afternoon. Miranda parked her car in front of the address Janet had written on the card, checked her lipstick, and stepped out into the snow. She had been to Petoskey a few times before, and found the office without any trouble. The building was two blocks past West Marine— a mix of residential homes and private offices. It was only thirty minutes from Charlevoix, a scenic drive along the lake.

The steps leading up to the restored craftsman bungalow were neatly shoveled and salted. Miranda stepped inside. "Mr. Tiller isn't in right now. Is there something I can help you with?" A receptionist named Rita was in her mid-fifties, pretty, with a southern accent. Miranda looked around. The lobby was understated and masculine, with a mid-century modern sofa and two Frank Lloyd Wright chairs that were worth thousands if they were authentic. The floors were beautifully refinished hardwood that glowed beneath the furniture. It was small but beautifully appointed. Even though she lived on an old boat, Miranda still liked nice things.

On the coffee table sat a large Murano art glass bowl, deeply saturated with shades of orange and red. It was filled with antique marbles that she recognized in an instant. Miranda felt a chill, a tingling that was no longer a pleasant sensation. She thought of Charlie Fine and wondered if this man could be a pirate, too. There were some modern paintings, pottery, and a life-size German Shepherd statue in the corner. *If the dog was there to scare people, Mr. Tiller had a lot to learn about security.*

Behind Rita there was an open door and a large office. Miranda saw framed photographs on the wall behind what she assumed was Tiller's desk. Maybe they would give her some indication about the nature of this business, but Rita was watching her closely. Miranda couldn't spot a single clue— not a sign or a logo, not a name on the mailbox or front door. There were no brochures or business cards neatly arranged on an end table— just the photographs in his office, and she was too far away to see them. Was that disturbing or exciting? Miranda could not be sure.

The reception desk was stylish, neat, and appointed with a computer, wide monitor, printer, and a complex phone system. A small black box with blinking lights was mounted off to one side. The cables and cords were meticulously dressed and disappeared into the floor, just like in Harry's office. Miranda was low tech, didn't even carry a cell phone. What on earth was Janet thinking?

Feeling a little deflated, she cleared her throat and told the receptionist that Janet had sent her. She hoped that name would carry some weight. Rita looked up and smiled. "Why, of course. Mr. Tiller will be happy to meet with you," and she scheduled an appointment for an interview. Rita took a business card from a chrome holder on her desk, wrote something on the back, and handed it to Miranda. The card had Rita's name and phone number but nothing else. Miranda handed Rita her resume and said she had just one question. "I hope I can help," Rita smiled.

"I was wondering if you could tell me a little bit about ..."

"Well of course! Mr. Tiller will be happy to talk with you about the nature of our work when it's time. And Miranda, just a word of advice. Be prepared, and don't be late." Miranda looked at the card in her hand. She was scheduled for an interview in two days!

"Better to be ordinary and work for a living than act important and starve in the process." Proverbs 12:9

Wednesday morning. Miranda arrived at her interview ten minutes early. She was greeted by Rita, offered coffee, and ushered into a large office, while the big, fake German Shepard looked on. Emerson James Tiller was seated at his desk holding her resume, a stack of newspapers and some file folders pushed off to one side. He stood up, introduced himself, and extended his hand. His handshake was firm, solid, and surprisingly warm for a cold day. Rather than offering her a seat, he asked her to remain standing and present her qualifications as if she were making a very important sale. At the time, Miranda had no idea how important this presentation would be.

Having spent the last 48 hours practicing what she would say, Miranda Stowe was ready. Since leaving Tiller's office on Monday, she gave her speech to anyone who would listen— her dockmates, the bartender at Jack's Steakhouse, and to herself in front of the mirror in the lady's room. With Neil Lipman loitering outside the door at his usual post, she hoped he was impressed. Miranda cleared her throat. She felt anxious and intimidated by this imposing man, but she was as prepared as she would ever be. Tiller said, "You may begin."

"Thank you, sir. My most recent employer was Stowe Publishing. The name is the same as my own because the company is owned by my former husband, Harry Stowe. This does not, in any way, diminish my contribution or success as it relates to my position there. As you may have noted, Harry Stowe is listed as a business reference, as well." She took a deep breath and was ready to continue, then glanced briefly over his shoulder at the pictures. Emerson James Tiller had the deportment of a State Highway Patrolman, hands neatly folded in front of him. He was watching her over the top of his reading glasses— possibly amused, probably not.

"I began my career with Stowe Publishing as an assistant editor and copywriter. I quickly gained a reputation for doing quality work, and completed writing assignments for a major market newspaper and several broadcast media outlets. I also did ghostwriting for a political candidate, preparing campaign speeches and correspondence. Each project eventually added to Stowe's bottom line by introducing local organizations to our complete printing and publishing services."

No response.

"As I gained experience, Harry included me in sales presentations on a broader scale. (She could feel herself missing Harry, and needed to stay focused.) I began to prospect and develop new accounts, working mostly with colleges and universities. I wrote proposals, studied needs-analysis data, and researched marketing trends. By building good relationships with my clients and being responsive to their needs, I was consistently recognized for bringing in the highest dollar volume of new business. I'm a strong negotiator, Mr. Tiller. I'm not ashamed to say I like making money."

Tiller looked down at her resume, wrote something on a legal pad, and said, "Continue."

"Like everyone else on the payroll, I was at the office anytime the workload demanded it. We operated as a team, and put out an exceptional product." Miranda paused. "If I may say so, Mr. Tiller, I loved my work, made a notable contribution, and look forward to achieving the same level of success with your firm." *(Level of success doing what? Miranda still had no idea what she was doing there.)*

Though she may have been a scotch drinker and a fun date, no one could ever criticize her talent or work ethic. And while she enjoyed those years she spent living a life of luxury with Harry Stowe, a girl can only buy so many sexy shoes and bags from the Louis Vuitton boutique. When she took a job at Harry's office, she never drank a drop— and she could do it again! She wanted to be responsible, and sober, and make her own way! Whatever this entailed, she wanted this job!

Miranda finished her presentation, not sure what was going to happen next. Tiller looked up from her resume and asked, trying to hide a grin, "About your volunteer position with the Orchid Society— Does that somehow relate to your work experience, or do you just like flowers?"

She met his gaze, relaxing a little, also trying not to grin. "When I became editor-in-chief of the Providence Orchid Society newsletter, I had never grown a plant in my life. But I'm a quick study, sir, and my orchids are thriving."

"And this makes you qualified to work for me."

"Yes Mr. Tiller, I believe it does."

Emerson James Tiller motioned for Rita to bring more coffee, and a folder with some papers for Miranda. Rita scheduled a second interview, and Miranda left, happy and still clueless.

As Miranda was leaving Petoskey to go back to Charlevoix, Neil Lipman was leaving Charlevoix to go to Traverse City. He had an important meeting with his brother-in-law, Joe Ramono. The lunch crowd at

Tommy's Gotcha was made up mostly of tradesmen, tourists during the season, and some day drinkers getting a head start on the weekend. Neil Lipman fit right in. There would be plenty of chatter and background noise, giving the men some privacy for a discrete conversation.

Attorney Joe Ramono always met with Neil at the local bar and grill because of Neil's heightened sense of clarity when he had a bucket of wings and a Bud Lite in front of him. He was at his best when his big belly was full and happy. Enjoying some fresh air with the window down, Lipman headed south out of Charlevoix in his old Ford F-150. He tapped his nicotine-stained fingers on the steering wheel, turned up the radio, and sang along with one of his favorite songs... *"Her name was Lola, she was a showgirl, with yellow feathers in her hair and a dress cut down to there..."* A cigarette dangled from the corner of his mouth.

Ramono was a stickler for being on time. "Time is money," he roared at Lipman, but Neil did not think it was healthy to be so uptight. That kind of pressure could give a man a heart attack! *"She would merengue, and do the cha-cha..."* He was already running ten minutes late, and would continue at his leisure, happily singing along. "When Joe sees what I've got on Miranda," Lipman sneered, "he'll be buying me drinks all day long!"

It's not that he didn't like Miranda per se, but he was being paid to keep an eye on her for a very important client. She could stand to be a little nicer to him, especially after he shoveled her out after the storm. Ramono got a taste of Miranda's high-spirited ways when she insisted it was Neil who robbed her boat over the Thanksgiving holiday. Ramono was Lipman's alibi, but Joe didn't like being involved— it was bad for business. Even though Miranda could be feisty at times, Neil needed to learn to deal with her. He needed to be more discreet.

Neil watched her out on the dock during the blizzard and wondered how she could survive— but she did. *She was a real cute girl when she put on some make-up and nice clothes to go out and hit the bars at night, he thought as he drove. Whoever was paying to have her watched must be extremely interested. It was costing somebody a lot of money for me to stand outside in the cold and smoke.*

Neil Lipman kept a log of all her daily activities, making note of who was coming and going, and running background checks on their cars in the parking lot. For a tomboy, Miranda sure had a lot of boyfriends. So he wrote everything down; those were the client's orders. Neil took a long drag on his cigarette, flicked the butt out the window, half of the ashes blowing back in. He glanced at the notebook on the seat beside him. Ramono's client was about to get his money's worth!

Neil Lipman pulled into a full parking lot at Tommy's Gotcha, just up the road from the Mallard Point Club. Neil could not picture that girl sitting on a bar stool at a fancy place. He laughed at the thought of her wearing that big trapper's hat, looking ridiculous. Neil often wondered if Miranda's ex-husband was "the client" who was paying to have her surveilled. Joe Ramono wouldn't say. Seated in the last booth on the right, the old red upholstery looked even more tattered than the last time he was there. Joe looked at his watch and greeted Neil with a curt, "You're late." There were chicken wings waiting on the table, and Neil tore into the bucket with delight. He licked his fingers while Joe reviewed the file. Joe was clearly impressed. "How did you get this?"

Neil was beaming. "I was stationed at my usual post next to the lady's room. Miranda was in there half the night, giving the same speech over and over. All I had to do was write it down."

"This is excellent work, Neil. Do you know what this means?"

Lipman ordered a beer. "I have no idea."

"Think about it, Neil... it's her resume! Miranda's applying for a job. And from the looks of things, she's a lot smarter than we gave her credit for." Three pretty girls entered the bar, Neil was distracted. "It explains how she designed that aft deck super structure overnight, and the extent of the modifications she must have done to make it through the storm. She's got a good head on her shoulders. The client saw her right over there at the bar. It was last fall. She was going on and on about anodized paint compounds, and bragging about her new orbital sander. Now that I think about it, she had paint on her nose." Joe did not mention she was drunk.

Neil shook his head. "For a girl, that's just plain weird." He held up his Bud Lite in a toasting gesture, and ordered the girls a round of drinks, on Joe.

"Maybe. But the client was curious. He walked around the bar, stood behind her, and listened to her talk like a pro about boat restoration. If Miranda would have turned around she would have bumped right into him."

Neil asked, "Where did ya hear that?"

"I was sitting beside her. She said she was leaving Mallard Point for Charlevoix in the morning, that she planned to live on her boat there all winter." Joe Ramono took a sip of his diet Coke. He never drank during the day.

Neil's eyes lit up, finally making the connection. "So the guy at the bar is the client?" Ramono would not say. "So why's he having her tailed? Is he up to no good? A stalker? A madman?

"He likes her, Neil. He's a rich guy who has the hots for a broad who lives on a boat. Happens all the time." Neil frowned, brushed the crumbs from his beard. "We set up the surveillance deal after she left. I put you on the job the very next day."

"And I was waiting at the Boat Basin when she motored in." Neil downed the rest of his beer. "Why doesn't he just ask her out on a date?"

Ramono looked at his watch. He had to be in court. "This guy doesn't operate that way. He's a big shooter. He wants information before he'll meet her face to face." Joe gestured to the waitress and asked for the check.

"So he's not a psycho."

"No, Neil."

"And I'm not a real P.I."

"You're an overpaid babysitter Neil, but so far you're doing a real good job." Ramono stood up laughing, slapped Neil on the back. "So where is she now?"

"I have no idea."

Seeking Miranda

Emerson James Tiller

Friday morning. Miranda sat alone in Tiller's office waiting for their meeting to begin, and more importantly, to find out whether she got the job. Rita brought her a cup of strong coffee and said her boss was on his way. She scanned the room, her eyes settling once again on the photos hanging behind Tiller's desk. She wondered how this man was able to avoid the prying eyes of the worldwide web. All of her internet searches for his name came up blank.

Although the pictures were taken years ago, Miranda instantly recognized the man in the pictures as James Tiller. He looked the same— black male, 6'4", muscular build, very handsome. There was a photo of him standing near the President as he threw out the first pitch. Another showed Tiller with the President jogging in the rain, flanked by his security detail. Next to that, a picture of the President and Billy Graham during an off-camera moment on the National Day of Prayer, with

Tiller in the background. (Miranda made a mental note— the President prays.) There was even a candid shot of the President with the Queen, Emerson James Tiller looking on. He was the only one in the picture not smiling.

As Miranda leaned forward to get a closer look, a voice interrupted her thoughts. "I was Secret Service Protective Detail for four years." Tiller walked past her, freshly polished shoes clicking with purpose across the hardwood floor. Rita brought a mug of coffee, a refill for Miranda, and took Tiller's wool topcoat without saying a word. Miranda stood up to shake his hand. "But before we get into all that, I see that Rita gave you some papers to review." Miranda opened the folder on her lap. "We need to go through them together."

Rita returned with a stack of newspapers and files, placed them on the credenza behind Tiller's desk, then left, closing the door behind her. "Page one," said Tiller, "is a standard confidentiality agreement. It restricts you from the use and dissemination of company owned confidential information, which means that everything you see and hear from this point forward is between us." Tiller continued. "A brief description of the organization is on page two, and an outline of the position I'm prepared to offer you follows."

Line by line she learned that Tiller's organization was called, *Special Services. (Special Services? That's it?)* The description read, in part, *"... conducts advance work and threat assessment, pinpointing vulnerabilities at locations with potential infrastructure and security breaches. Special Services determines, designs, and installs appropriate technologies and countermeasures to ensure maximum event protection, then assesses our own performance to improve operations in the future. This service applies to the protectee and the event's general population."*

"So if the Rolling Stones are doing a show at the Chicago Pavilion, Ms. Stowe, we can secure the facility by land and along the shoreline, protect the band, and protect those in attendance. We can prevent nearly any incident before it occurs. We protect celebrities, entertainers, professional athletes, and national dignitaries, to name a few." Miranda blinked hard and was speechless.

Tiller scribbled something on a legal pad and turned it around on his desk for her to see. It was a dollar figure. "You'll learn more as we go along. And according to my research, you're qualified for the job. Are you interested?" Miranda knew it was important not to react, but to remain calm and professional. On the inside, she was high five-ing herself and doing back flips in the parking lot. But on the outside, she put on her best poker face and narrowed her eyes to hide her excitement. Tiller added, "That's before commissions and bonuses."

Miranda knew she had just caught the brass ring of a lifetime. She thought about Janet, and her friend Mavis who always prayed for her. Then she calmly cleared her throat and replied, "Thank you sir, I accept."

"I look forward to having you on board, Ms. Stowe."

"I'm looking forward to it as well. And please call me Miranda."

"In that case, you can call me Tiller." He stood up, shook her hand, and almost smiled.

Miranda left Petoskey after her meeting with Tiller, singing "Bohemian Rhapsody"— the opera section— louder than usual. Back in Charlevoix, she stopped at Jack's Steakhouse and ordered a Rueben sandwich for lunch, not even thinking about a cold beer. (So far, there were no shakes, sweats, or cravings. Giving up alcohol wasn't as hard as she thought.)

Before she left the office, Tiller said she would need a proper business wardrobe, several suits in case she was working out-of-town and needed to stay over. He offered her an advance against her pay, enough to buy her favorite labels, plus tasteful shoes and a conservative handbag. Miranda trembled with excitement, praying that her new job would not get off to a reckless, manic start.

She finished one last greasy fry, headed down to the Boat Basin, and greeted Neil Lipman who was smoking by the lady's room. Miranda ducked inside, took off her black pumps and delicate ultra-sheer hose, then carried them down the dock barefoot, determined not to fall and damage her nice accessories. Even though the snow had melted, the dock was really cold. "Have you lost your mind, Miranda? Finally snapped? The shoes go on your *feet*, not on your *hands*." Luke hiked up his jeans revealing L.L. Bean duck boots to prove his point.

"Hi Luke," she blew him a kiss and smiled. He hated it when she was nice to him.

Ron shouted, "Hey, where have you been? It's not like you to roll out of bed before noon."

"I got a job, Ron! A really good job, and I start Monday!"

"I can't believe it, Miranda," Luke bellowed. "You mean someone actually fell for that fake resume?" She winked.

"It isn't fake."

"Is to."

"Is not! I'm going aboard my boat now, Luke, because my toes are freezing, and I'm not in the mood." She said it in a deep, sexy voice.

"Yeah, sure. Just remember Monday morning not to show up at work barefoot. Even your fake resume won't get you out of that one."

As Luke's words faded like a distant clanging gong, Miranda counted out her lithium pills on the counter. Her days of skipping doses were over. She pulled on her brown work boots, an unstylish look with her suit, and climbed out of her boat with all her bottles. The dockmates took the liquor off her hands, impressed that she was willing to give up her stash. Maybe there was hope for their friend after all.

It was Miranda's birthday, and besides landing a job, she couldn't think of a better place to celebrate than Grand Traverse Mall with the money from Tiller. Shopping always made her think of Harry. He had such good taste, and loved to see her all dressed up. She wished he was there to help her pick out some new clothes for work, then take her home to model her new birthday suit.

With an armload of proper clothes still on the hangers and several glossy shopping bags, Miranda returned to her boat rejoicing. Although it was dark, something drew her out to the very end of the pier. She sat quietly, feet dangling off the edge, and looked out into the cold. With limited experience praying to anyone, including the ambiguous "Higher Power" of Alcoholics Anonymous, she took a moment to thank God. Though she didn't know Him well, she hoped He was listening.

The mornings were cold and the pier was long. Miranda carried her good shoes down the dock in a tote bag, driving through the ice and snow on her way to work. Spring was nowhere in sight. She thought about the Bible and the verses she had been reading lately; she was grateful to have a good job. But sometimes she wondered: If God is good, why did he allow her boat to get robbed? Was she being punished for all the money she got from Charlie Fine? And if taking money from Charlie was really that bad, why did God drop the perfect job right in her lap so she could get more? Miranda had a lot of questions...

She liked going to the office. While her official title was "Special Projects Manager," she was basically Tiller's assistant. Wherever he went, Miranda followed with a clipboard, cell phone, and a lipstick called *Blaze,* a bold new shade that promised to take the business world by storm. Nars Jungle Red was a little too sassy for the workplace, and she wanted to look professional. After months of being bundled up in boyish flannel and her trapper's hat, she was happy to see a pretty girl looking back at her in the mirror. Never again would the lady at the Wendy's drive-thru hand her a cheeseburger and say, "Thank you, sir."

Miranda often stayed late at the office to study products used in various installations— the technology was complicated. One rainy night, she was curled up with a technical manual and a big bag of Cheetos on her desk. She was studying biometric technology for access control, compared to *biodynamic signature technology* which incorporated both genetic and physiological elements.

It was hard to imagine access recognition based on breathing and brain activity— even scary in a way— but Tiller evidently had a client who was interested, and she wanted to be prepared. Miranda figured if she could learn how to rewire an old boat without killing herself, maybe she could understand this, too. She made a mental note to get that old fuse box looked at by a professional— it was long overdue.

Deciphering all the complex diagrams made Miranda sleepy and her thoughts began to drift. She wondered about Charlie. She felt dirty and damaged by all of the things she did with him, all the money he gave her, and all the secrets she kept. Did he make her *a prostitute?* Or did she willingly take on that role? If she were to be perfectly honest with herself, she would just admit that for all those times they were together, she was in love with a man who treated her that way. She tried not to think about it.

The heavy book slipped off her lap and went crashing to the floor, but Miranda hardly noticed. Her arrangement with Charlie was simple at first— nice restaurants, gifts, fancy hotel rooms. She *loved* being in bed with him, but in the days that followed the guilt was unbearable. It was only after she and Harry divorced that Miranda actually needed the money. On the nights Charlie stayed on her boat, he woke up early and always left a stack of bills on the counter. He said he did it because he cared about her, and she believed him.

She wondered about Evelyn Fine, so pretty and kind. She thought about their friends at Mallard Point. Surely someone at the club must have suspected something! The Parkers and the Pewterschmidts were his neighbors out on B dock, and he vacationed on the island last winter with the Hubbards and the Howells. Had Harry not been such a workaholic, they would have been invited, too. Besides, when he was away, Charlie called every day, which would have been impossible if his wife was there. She considered that for a moment.

Didn't anyone know he was married? Miranda ate some Cheetos and licked the orange powder off her fingers, lamenting all that she'd gone through. Had no one ever seen Evelyn Fine at the club, or the pool, or at Tommy's Gotcha? She thought about all of the security measures at his boat. She was so busy playing with his toys and drinking his scotch that she never put the pieces together. Charlie Fine was a liar and a cheat. Miranda was happy to finally know the truth.

She remembered how it seemed so intimate when they shared a dinner and appetizer, nibbling bites of lobster off the same plate. If Charlie's wife looked at his credit card statements, an expensive dinner for two would have looked pretty suspicious. And what about all the electronic gadgets Miranda wasn't allowed to touch? And why two cell phones? Charlie's money made her feel secure at the time, but now it made her feel foolish. Miranda ate the last Cheeto and cried.

Her melancholy was dragging her down the same old path, always leading back to thoughts of Harry. She couldn't deny that his wealth from the publishing business gave her a sense of security, or how grand it was to live like a queen and go shopping every day. Moving from a suburban palace to the frozen tundra of Lake Michigan taught her that she was strong and resourceful, and could ride out any storm. She learned about courage, friendship, and how to use power tools.

She didn't know what her future would bring, but whatever it was, she knew she would make it. Though no one could ever take Harry's place, Miranda wondered if she might meet someone and get married again someday. But since she worked late every night and didn't have a boyfriend, that was not an immediate concern.

It was late. She looked at the manual at her feet, the pages crumpled. She licked her fingers and picked up the book, leaving an orange thumbprint on the table of contents. She would deal with that later. Miranda knew she needed to make amends to Harry. It was something she learned about when she went to AA meetings with Lydia. Everyone said it was a healthy thing to do, and it actually helped people stay sober. Though she didn't expect him to accept her apology, telling him how sorry she was, was the right thing to do. She would call Harry, and she would do it soon.

Maybe reading her Bible was changing the way she looked at things. There was a Baptist church on the square a few blocks from the Boat Basin. But Miranda had some bad experiences at church as a kid, and even worse situations later. She was looking for God's forgiveness not judgment and condemnation. Church was a scary place— but she sure couldn't figure things out on her own.

"Don't worry about anything; instead pray about everything. Tell God what you need, and thank him for all he has done." Philippians 4:6

The Kiss

By the time spring arrived on Lake Michigan, Miranda had settled into a nice routine at work. In the past months, Tiller wrote a proposal for a metropolitan shopping village under construction in West Palm Beach, installed surveillance equipment at a decommissioned NASA nuclear research facility (undisclosed location, of course), and sent a team to do a security upgrade at Wisconsin State Fair Park. The Judds were doing a show that summer and the organizers wanted everything to be perfect. The fair drew over a million people each year and the concert was expected to be a sellout. While it was impossible to predict every theoretical security breach, Tiller was the best in the business, and Miranda was honored to carry his clipboard.

Back on Miranda's boat, however, there were complications. Most of the repairs she made prior to the winter season were holding up well. Her fuse box upgrade, however, was not. It seemed that some electrical gremlins had made their way into the fuse box, making it impossible for her to do two things at once: hairdryer + microwave, stereo + curling iron, space heaters + television, or any combination of the above. She was living like the Amish and started to hate it.

Miranda stopped at the marina office and told the clerk that she had a technician coming in to make a repair. She was sure Drew Becker could fix it. He had a great reputation up and down Michigan's west coast working on everything from old woodies to upgrading electronics on the finest boats. When Miranda first met him at Tommy's Gotcha last fall, he was installing a huge navigation package on a yacht that hadn't left the dock all summer. The owner, a Greek millionaire (and apparently a drunk), needed it to stroke his ego and whatever else— fairly typical for the money crowd.

The boat was called *Neptune's Hammer*, down on E dock at Mallard Point. Miranda said it didn't ring a bell. Becker told her to call if she needed any work done on her boat, adding that he would work for beer and pizza. She batted her eyes, feigned her most alluring damsel in distress, and said she didn't need *anyone*, but thanks. At least that was her plan. The Boat Basin was starting to come to life, and boats were slowly being launched. She was elated that spring was finally here! Miranda sprinted up the ramp to the marina building, greeted the man at the service desk and told him her plans. Before she could finish, an unpleasant sound came bellowing from the manager's office.

"I'm asking you a question, Miranda. Who is the technician?" A stout woman with a face like a bulldog stepped out of her office and approached Miranda at the counter. Her name was Kelly; Miranda didn't like her, and the feeling was mutual.

"Drew Becker," Miranda said with a dreamy look in her eyes, batting her eyelashes for effect. She knew Kelly had a crush on him and did this to annoy her.

"Miranda, you know the rules about using outside contractors. If he's not on our list, I can't approve him to come in. Besides, Drew's working down in the Keys." Kelly thought she knew everything.

"I know... I've missed him." Miranda was enjoying this little exchange.

"But you said he was fixing your boat."

"He just got back. I can't wait to see him!" She winked.

Kelly looked over the top of her thick round glasses and glared at her. "He doesn't seem like your type, Miranda."

"Trust me, he's all that... and more."

"Well, the policy states that only approved contractors, family, and significant others are allowed to work on boats, so if he *really is* your boyfriend, I guess I'll have to allow it." She looked defeated, poor Kelly.

Miranda beamed. She grabbed her cell phone and dialed, dodging Neil Lipman on her way down the ramp. "Drew... Hi. Listen... when you come over tonight go straight down the ramp and meet me at the gate. Yeah, they're giving me a hard time. When I get down there, grab me, pull me close, and kiss me like you mean it. They need to think you're my boyfriend." Although Drew was still in his work clothes— not exactly dressed for a date— he couldn't wait to see how this one turned out.

An hour later, they met at the gate. He grabbed her, pulled her close, and kissed her hard, just as she asked. Miranda was stunned, realized it had been a long time since anyone kissed her that way. She reminded herself to exhale. Drew picked up his tools, ignored her, and headed down the pier. He was all business. Miranda ran to keep up. *What the heck... that's it? He's not even gonna hit on me? Is he gay?!*

Drew climbed aboard the old Marinette and unpacked his tools— a fuse puller, wire cutters, fish tape, and a bag of Oreos. He offered her a cookie. She stood staring at him, her cheeks burning. She took half a stack out of the package and reached in the fridge for some milk— apparently, they were both hungry.

Miranda made small talk and watched him work. Drew was a tall, barrel chested man with broad shoulders, long legs, and big muscular arms, probably played sports in school. He had on a ball cap that said NYU, worn baggie jeans, and work shoes. While she was not the blue-collar type, she found him appealing.

As Drew unscrambled a few decades of bad wiring, Miranda noticed his hands, rough and very large. She asked about Key West, his plans for the summer. When she got up to take a look at his work, Drew stepped behind her and leaned in close. She felt a spark— a jolt that ran all the way to her toes! He explained the problem and the repairs he had made, pointing out that she actually did a pretty good job for a beginner.

Miranda could not ignore the heat of his body pressing against her. The grease under his fingernails and the distinct smell of diesel fuel were strangely intoxicating. She felt his breath on her neck. With the fuse box replaced, Miranda thanked him and said goodnight. Drew picked up his tools, Miranda blushed. Something felt awkward. Maybe kissing the technician on the dock wasn't such a good idea after all, because now she wanted him to kiss her again. He climbed off the aft deck and disappeared into the night. He said, "Call me if you need anything..."

The Stadium

Miranda crawled out from under a sea of flannel sheets, the electric blanket, a silk chenille throw, and a down comforter stuffed inside a soft duvet. She toasted toast, curled her hair, and put on Vivaldi's *The Four Seasons,* Concerto No. 4 in F minor, Op. 8, called "*Winter,*" the Largo movement.

A virtuoso plays passionately. Miranda sipped her coffee and listened. *A quiet rhythm takes cautious steps; the cellos enter on tiptoes... waiting, waiting... lingering in that melodic place a little while.* Miranda was feeling distracted. *There is a sense that the song has a secret, something erotic, something to hide. Is that a crescendo? A warmth where there was none before? Anticipation is turning to impatience, demanding to know what is coming. Now! Now! A downbeat, a crescendo!! The violins are caught off guard, their melody is exquisite and reaching. Finally, the tension is broken!*

There was a crash, a shudder, a fierce drawn-out sigh. Miranda's cheeks were on fire... it was better than she imagined. She was thinking about Drew.

As much as she would like to, Miranda couldn't hang around and listen to Vivaldi all day. She gathered up her things for the trip, Miranda always over packed. Zipping closed her suitcase, she grabbed her handbag, climbed off the boat, and carried her good shoes to the parking lot. She left her boat relieved that her electrical worries were over. Her craving for another Oreo, however, was not.

Miranda watched for Tiller's BMW. He was picking her up at the Boat Basin for a security project out of town. Ordinarily, they chartered a plane out of the small municipal airport in Harbor Springs, or flew commercial from Detroit. But Tiller just bought a new car and was eager to take it for a ride. Miranda loved a good road trip and was excited to be going with him. Their destination: a college football stadium in Ohio. A controversial former first lady was scheduled to give the commencement address. Spring graduation was just ten weeks away; heightened security was paramount. According to Miranda's calculations, their destination was 443 miles from Charlevoix, six hours fifty-two minutes according to the map, and roughly five-and-a-half hours Tiller time.

The University already had a reputation for rigorous screening of fans on game day, with every small detail checked and scrutinized. While a man carrying a gun is more dangerous than a man carrying a half empty water bottle, the risk is still noteworthy. Long lines and impatient fans were sometimes the result, but safety had to come first. Tiller had done work on the campus before, and looked forward to crawling around the massive concrete behemoth, affectionately known as, *The Shoe.* He admired the school's commitment to maintaining the highest security levels possible. And while it was never his intent to scare a client into spending more than necessary, Tiller was aware that the university's Athletic Department brought in more money than any other college in the nation. They are the elite. The school demanded the best, and only *Special Services* could provide it.

Tiller accelerated and told Miranda to hang on. He was winding out the gears, but the car hardly made a sound. She wondered if he ever drove the President. Since she was experiencing his driving skills for the first time, she wondered if the President ever got nervous, too. "First, we will contract with the nation's best snipers and place them strategically throughout the stadium. I have a source for that. Most will be in plain clothes and virtually undetectable.

There will be an advance team with specially trained dogs to sniff out explosives and sweep the facility at scheduled intervals. The last one will be at 0800-hours just prior to the event. Every door in the stadium—hundreds of doors, Miranda— has to be unlocked, and each room checked for explosives. When it's all clear, each door is *re-locked* and taped. Scoreboards and ribbon boards will be pre-programmed with instructions, shelter information, and where to go for triage in the event of a true emergency."

She could hear the anticipation in his voice— Tiller loved this stuff! "Joint efforts by national security, state and local police, as well as the school's Special Services unit will be on hand throughout the day. An exclusive group of ushers known as "Red Coats" play an important role in seating and managing the crowd, and will be thoroughly briefed for the event. They are the eyes and ears of stadium activity, more than one hundred members strong, and stationed at every level. They know the lay of the land, Miranda, and they take their work as seriously as trained professionals." A client once asked Tiller how to assess the return on his company's security investment. Tiller calmly replied, "Count the bodies, my friend... just count the bodies."

Miranda was starving and it was only ten o'clock in the morning. Tiller hated to waste time eating lunch, or meals in general. "Worst potential disaster, Miranda?" It was a rhetorical question. "It would have to be a fire on game day. Try to imagine the catastrophic reaction of 100,000 people fleeing their seats and rushing toward a crowded concourse already filled with smoke. People on ramps and stairways would be trampled and burned to death. Thousands would die; the loss of life would be tremendous. And that doesn't even include the people in the upper decks falling to their deaths— or jumping." He shuddered.

Stadium attacks were ranked as one of the twelve most devastating acts of terrorism according to

Miranda's research. It made her troubles with Neil Lipman and getting robbed on her boat seem small. She was glad she packed enough clothes to stay the week. Their work here would take some time. Tiller took a sip out of a half full bottle of water, his wheels still turning. Heading up the ramp and merging onto I-75, a long Mayflower moving van roared past Tiller's car, cutting him off without warning and kicking up a few small stones. He was aghast!

After mumbling a few choice words, he straightened his sunglasses, cleared his throat, and asked Miranda if she had ever loaded and moved a house full of furniture. *Seriously?* She rolled her eyes and said she had not. "Wanna hear a story about the time me and my buddy Raymond loaded the biggest moving van you've ever seen?" Was Tiller about to trust her with more presumably classified information? It was a side of her boss she hadn't expected to see— ever. The ride to Columbus, Ohio would be more interesting than she imagined.

"On a good day, enjoy yourself; On a bad day, examine your conscience. God arranges for both kinds of days So that we won't take anything for granted." Ecclesiastes 7:14

"We were doing a moving job for a family that bought a cottage up north at Wequetonsing... you know, right there across the bay from the office. It was going to be their 'summer home,' as if a boy from the projects knew what that meant." Miranda laughed. He said 'summer home' imitating the voice of a snooty rich woman. Miranda knew the type— this was hilarious! "In my neighborhood growing up, you were lucky to have a home, period! And we lived in that same house all year long, all four seasons, and always with a bunch of relatives, too. Imagine that!"

"I got into the moving business the summer I turned 14... the pay was real good. Raymond— my cousin Raymond— got me the job, lied about my age, told 'em I was older. So we worked all day in the heat— I had never seen so much fine stuff! Then we carried out the last piece... an old baby grand piano that had to come off the truck first the next day. And there was just enough room. I was a real skinny kid, and that piano was HEAVY!"

Tiller looked like he had traveled back 40 years and was reliving that day in the driver's seat of his new $80,000 car. He explained how he wiped the sweat off his face with his dirty undershirt, then walked into town to buy a Coke and some chips. The time and temperature sign at the bank said 101-degrees. Miranda was enjoying his candor. Tiller was a real person after all.

"When I got back to the truck, I folded up a stack of moving blankets and climbed into the cab to sleep. In the morning we would deliver the furniture to the biggest cottage you've ever seen, right on the lake with a covered boat dock. Had to be worth millions even in those days." Tiller passed an SUV with a GO BUCKS bumper sticker and a bunch of clean-cut midwestern looking kids packed inside. Miranda knew they were getting close.

Tiller continued. "I tried to get comfortable so I could sleep, but the blankets were dirty and damp with my own sweat. While I was lying there, Miranda, there was one thing I knew: I did not want to do hard physical work like that ever again in my whole life. I saw all that good furniture, the paintings, and that damned heavy piano, and I saw my future. If I worked harder than anyone else, I would be successful, too." At age 14, Emerson James Tiller didn't know how right he was.

"We finished the job the next day, made it back to Detroit. I headed straight for the bowling alley where I set pins on the weekends. The money wasn't great, but it was steady. I was the man of the house, you know... helpin' my mom take care of me and my sisters. Between that and stocking shelves at the grocery store, we managed to make ends meet." He took another sip of water, checked the rear-view mirror to make a lane change. "You're not asleep over there, are you Miranda?" She could hear the smile in his voice.

"On weekends, the lanes were busy, and I could always count on some extra tips above what they paid me." Tiller told her a story about some gamblers who came in late on Saturday nights and always stayed past closing— laughing, drinking, and betting on who would win the next game. They wore dark suits, gold rings, and smelled like whiskey! "When the stakes got high, the owner left me with the keys and those crazy men stayed and bowled all night! Not only did I earn my regular pay, but an extra $20 tip and a few free beers! I always made out okay. The point is Miranda, my priorities were already in place. Set goals, work hard, and make money."

"That must have been very hard," she sighed. Miranda looked at his hands, swollen and gnarled against the steering wheel. She thought about those bowling balls crashing against them. She always assumed it was arthritis.

"Hard? Are you kidding me? You know what—you've got it made out there on that boat of yours, livin' the "Life of Riley!" She had no idea what he was talking about, and she didn't know anyone named Riley. But knowing Tiller, he was probably right.

It was after 2:00pm when they arrived in Columbus. Tiller cruised the perimeter of the old football stadium, then made his way to Gate 23, a secured entrance used for day-to-day business and deliveries. A sleepy student with acne looked away from his phone and asked Tiller for his ID. He yawned, rubbed his eyes, and handed Tiller a clipboard, gesturing to the place where he should sign in. The student made a note, handed back Tiller's driver's license, and waved them in. As the boy turned back to his reading, Tiller handed the ID to Miranda. It belonged to her coworker, a computer guy right out of school named Evan. His short blond hair and freckles were a dead giveaway that he was not a 58-year-old black man. Tiller rolled his eyes, Miranda made a note. He would have preferred an armed guard with an assault rifle, security cameras, and a drooling German Shepherd— an ounce of prevention, he called it.

They drove through the gate and crept along at idle speed, looking for the area where Tiller's contact told him to park. The sprawling cement concourse was lined with snack shops on one side, kiosks for soda, T-shirts, and giant pretzels on the other. They were empty and abandoned— hibernating till fall. Tiller stopped at the end of the drive where the concourse met a long ramp. They stepped out of the car. The stadium smelled like wet sneakers. A dark echo and the click-clicking of Miranda's heels led them into another gated area where steel support beams crossed over head.

The famous field was not yet in view. They were met by a broad-shouldered man in his sixties. He was muscular, with big hands and a bald head. Except for a neatly trimmed goatee, he was proper and clean-shaven like someone in the military. The man's name was McDevitt. He flashed a badge, a gun, and a wide smile, then threw open his arms and reached for Tiller. "Bring it in brother, bring it in!" Tiller returned the greeting, slapping McDevitt on the back as they broke out in riotous laughter, calling each other names that only old friends could. By the time Tiller introduced Miranda she was speechless.

They followed McDevitt up, up, up a wide concrete structure, a spiral path winding its way to the top of the stadium. It was open and visible from the vast parking lot on the other side. This must have been one of the areas Tiller was talking about, a place that would be most dangerous if the stadium had to be evacuated. As if Miranda was reading her bosses mind, he gestured and said, "Make a note." Protocol was restored to business as usual.

Miranda lagged behind, hoping to catch a glimpse of the field, and also, because her feet were killing her! The Stuart Weitzman's had a shiny red heel and more red leather where her toes peeked through. Normally they were fabulous—*almost* too sexy for work, but not quite! Today they just hurt! She made a note, ha ha. It was actually worth getting blisters just to be out of Charlevoix for a few days, glad to be away from the omniscient gaze of Neil Lipman, lingering like a virus on a dark night.

They stopped for a moment so Tiller could make a call. Miranda spotted a lady's room and dashed inside. There were at least 20 stalls, half as many sinks, and trash cans stationed all over the place. Women could be real pigs when they got drunk at football games—sometimes she missed those days. The absence of Neil's prying eyes was refreshing, knowing that nobody was judging her outfit, or taking notes, or listening to her pee.

They took an elevator to the press box level— finally! The view from the top was amazing! Tiller and McDevitt both agreed that a biometric signature ID system would add an extra layer of security to the control center and the people who ran the show. It's a place that a terrorist would likely target. Miranda was glad she studied all those technical manuals and asked a lot of questions ahead of time. She had come a long way and was grateful. As she followed Tiller's eyes waiting for his next instruction, she spotted a fat man seated across the field—feet up, smoking a cigarette, and enjoying the view. She froze. His name growled like a beast in her throat, a cigarette waiting to be snuffed out forever! IT WAS LIPMAN!!

Miranda had been a fool to think his presence in her life was a mere coincidence, or that she was in no danger. She did not care what anybody said, she knew Joe Ramono was in on it, and maybe some of his drinking buddies, too! When she got back from Columbus, she decided a trip to Tommy's Gotcha was in order. One of the men at the bar would know something. She made enough money that she could buy rounds all night if she had to. She would get someone to talk.

It was also time to ask her boss for his help. Miranda hated to open up her personal life to Jim Tiller, but on her own she had accomplished nothing. McDevitt led them back down the elevator to the field. Tiller sensed her unease and gestured for her to stay close. Miranda took one last look across the field— Lipman was gone!

Back at Tommy's

Once back in Charlevoix, Miranda had a decision to make. She had stayed sober all this time. There was no way she could have completed her work on the stadium project had she been hitting the campus bars at night. She counted up the months and days: January to May, four months and 16 days, all without Alcoholics Anonymous, a shrink, or any other support group. There were nights when she missed going out, but Tiller worked her so hard that she didn't have time anyway.

On May fifteenth, her winter dockage at the Boat Basin would run out— it was time to move on. Once the marina manager learned that Miranda was not really dating Drew Becker, and for that matter, hardly even knew him, life on the dock had changed. Kelly had been duped and Miranda would pay! But she was ready to leave the Boat Basin and move a little closer to work.

Miranda's plan was to run the old Marinette up the shoreline and east into Little Traverse Bay, the prettiest place on all the Great Lakes! The town of Harbor Springs was on the north side, protected to the west by a mile-long peninsula called Harbor Point. Wequetonsing, Labre Croache, and Bay View followed the shoreline around to the town of Petoskey. She would spend the summer at the city docks there. Miranda would not miss walking down the long pier through wind, ice, and snow to get to her job each day. What on earth was she thinking?

All of the dockmates volunteered to make the trip with her. To his surprise, she asked Luke. And to Miranda's surprise, he accepted. Ron was moving in with a lady he met at Jack's Steakhouse, and would be taking the boat down to Glen Arbor. Greg was planning an extended trip through the Straits of Mackinaw, down through Lake Huron to Lake Erie, and finally out the Welland Canal. From there he would travel north to Rhode Island where he would meet up with his estranged boyfriend and hopefully work out their differences. She had grown to adore Greg, and wished him all the best.

Miranda enjoyed the ride to Petoskey, and she could tell that Luke did, too. Turns out he wasn't really a jerk after all. As the youngest of five brothers, he learned that having a big mouth was a matter of survival, and after that, it just stuck. Toward the end of their time as dockmates, Miranda caught on and pegged him as one of the good guys. She was glad he was there with her on Lake Michigan that morning. As they motored north, the seas grew rough and Miranda spotted a dead head off to port. A collision with the huge log would have been devastating. No problem for Luke. Confident at the helm, he avoided a crash.

Under the roar of the engines, Miranda reflected on her visit to Tommy's Gotcha following her week at The Shoe. It was the last time she would try to learn more about Neil Lipman and the trouble he was causing in her life. After that, Tiller agreed to take over.

Miranda recalled that it was a humid night in Traverse City, and she was ready for a confrontation. Tommy's was lined with the same old faces, the same men who toasted her when she left town last fall. Joe Ramono was supposed to be one of the good guys, looking out for the drunken patrons, then charging a life's savings to get them off the hook. Her respect for him had waned. Vince, the imaginary cowboy, shouted, "Howdy there, little lady," tipping his ten-gallon hat like a true imaginary gentleman. His sidekick, Lester, pounded his fists on the bar, yelling at the waitress for another Bud Lite. They were still quite a pair.

Drew Becker had on a faded T-shirt, probably came straight from work. He grinned and winked at her, probably still thinking about Oreo cookies and how badly he wanted her. She held his glance a second too long, and smiled.

Two seats over, the man in the navy blue blazer followed her with his eyes from the moment she walked in. He nodded and said, "Hello, Miranda," and invited her to sit down, his date nowhere in sight. Ever since she bumped into him that day at the airport, she was curious about the allusive, well dressed stranger. He was probably just another rich, successful guy in a blazer, looking for the right girl to compliment his lavish lifestyle— a shiny new jewel in his imaginary crown. Miranda was glad her days as "arm candy" were over. She wondered if Drew knew him...

At the end of the bar sat Charlie Fine. There was a young blond on his lap, twirling her hair and sipping a pink girlie cocktail through a straw. She wore a sheer white T-shirt and a short denim skirt, and giggled as she tried to tie a knot in the cherry stem between her teeth. Charlie's eyes were at half mast, his pirate lips kissing his way down the girl's throat. He stroked her hair, seducing her with his shiny hook. Miranda hated the thought of this person spending the night on Charlie's boat, sleeping on her side of the bed in the master stateroom. The strap of a black bra peaked out of her shirt... no class whatsoever. If she hated Charlie so much, why did she even care? She dabbed her eyes and moved on. She was there on business, and she wasn't leaving without some answers.

After an aggressive interrogation of everyone at the bar, she learned absolutely nothing about Neil Lipman. She tried to question Mitzi the chronic day drinker, and her friend who brought along a standard poodle. The dog lapped water from his own shiny bowl; the women insisted they knew nothing.

The faces at the bar looked at each other, scratched their heads, and played dumb as if they had rehearsed for that very moment. Charlie's friend with the pink cocktail batted her eyes. Then, as if history was about to repeat itself, Miranda said goodbye, got in her car, and left Traverse City forever.

Hi Harry, it's me

Miranda had been saving her money and decided it was time to buy a house. Life at the Petoskey City Marina was a disaster. Disorderly drunks and loud sailors roamed the docks day and night. There was alcohol everywhere. She found herself missing the quiet beauty of Lake Charlevoix and especially her dockmates. Miranda could not wait to get out of there! One morning, as a tribe of undisciplined children shot bottle rockets off her swim platform, Miranda sat reading the local paper. According to the business section, interest rates were at an all-time low. She sipped her coffee, studied the fine print, and thought about the money she had in the bank. Maybe it was enough to buy a home of her own.

She scanned the real estate section, called an agent, and set up a time to look at some houses. She fell in love with the very first one, made an offer, and moved in two weeks later. Buying a house was like getting married—

a serious commitment, but without the ring and the cake. Miranda didn't like to waste time making important decisions. Better to trust your instincts and jump right in! But unlike her marriages to Brian Parker Hall and Harry Stowe, this choice turned out to be perfect.

With the same joy she found in restoring her old boat, her projects around the house were a labor of love. Woodwork was stripped of its thick painted layers, stain and varnish were carefully applied. Wood floors were brought back to their original beauty, and the kitchen countertops were covered with broken pieces of polished glass and tile, carefully grouted, creating a magical collage of color and shine. It helped that Drew Becker, with his power tools and strong hands was experienced with this sort of thing.

Something happened that last night at Tommy's Gotcha. Miranda didn't leave the bar alone. Drew Becker walked out right after she did and followed her to her car. She hoped he had some information about Neil Lipman, something he didn't want to reveal in front of the others. He asked if she wanted to get a drink at Deeny's Hideaway. Drew ordered a beer, Miranda a diet Coke. She was still sober and faithfully took her lithium every day. But lately she was feeling restless, staying up late at night, thinking about her house. She recognized these symptoms and knew it was a bad sign.

Visions of paint colors, draperies, and expensive leather furniture began swirling into beautifully appointed rooms. She hung the Tarkay, glad that Harry let her keep it in the divorce, and grateful it survived the winter in a Charlevoix gallery. Harry never liked the ladies anyway. Thoughts of the painting were always the sign of a brewing storm, a manic episode waiting to strike. With Miranda so busy at work, and now with the house, there was really no time to address it. And because mania's drama and power feel so good, she secretly invited it to stay. The ladies were in agreement; they approved.

While Drew Becker enjoyed his second beer at Deeny's, Miranda told him all about her new home, and Drew told Miranda all about the old boat house. They finished their drinks, finished their stories. Drew said if she ever needed an extra set of hands on a project she should call him. He handed her a crumpled business card from his back pocket. While she wasn't about to admit it, she still had the card he gave her that night on her boat, and it had nothing to do with her breaker box.

Miranda needed to start getting to bed earlier, maybe drink some warm milk and spend more time at the gym. It was getting harder to get up for work. Her bursts of energy were now accompanied by anxiety and agitation. Her symptoms didn't feel as good as she remembered. Miranda didn't want Tiller to know. He had done so much for her, and she would never want to let him down. And now that she was becoming friends with Drew Becker, she had to get her emotions under control.

But secretly, she knew what was happening. This was not an imaginary condition that she could ignore or wish away. She knew there were doctors and medications that could help her, save her from whatever consequences lie ahead. But the spinning of her thoughts began to feel familiar— like the highest hill on a roller coaster, hands in the air, screaming at the sky! And this time Miranda wanted to be in the front seat. It was not an accident; it was her choice.

Miranda set up her paint roller and tray, moved a small wooden ladder, and rearranged the drop cloth. It was Friday. She had the day off and a busy weekend planned. Miranda had become quite a prolific painter and was making fast progress working from room to room on the first floor. She stopped for lunch, washed her hands, and looked in the bathroom mirror. She grinned and wiped away a spot of red paint from her nose. Harry would have found that delightful. Miranda picked up the phone and dialed. She had put off calling him long enough.

"Hi Harry, it's me."

"Miranda... it's good to hear your voice. How are you?"

"I'm good."

"Are you still living aboard your boat?"

"I sold it. I finished the restoration and sold it on the day that everything worked."

Harry laughed. "I knew you could do it, Miranda... I've always believed in you."

"Thanks, Harry."

"So if you're not on your boat, where are you?"

"I'm in my dining room. In my house."

"Your house?"

"My house!"

Silence on the line.

"Harry...?"

"I'm here, Hun." He sounded confused. "It's just that I can't believe... *you bought a house?"*

More silence...

"So Miranda... you're working?"

"Yes. I have a good job."

"That's wonderful news!"

Harry was humoring her, just like he did when they were together— Miranda soaking in the tub up to her ears in bubbles, Harry still gorgeous after a long day at work. He was so good to her. Miranda needed to stay focused. She was still struggling to put those memories behind her.

"And what kind of work do you do?"

"It's classified, Harry, I can't tell you. Let's just say I'm in sales."

"And do you get to wear pretty clothes every day? And nice shoes?"

"I'm all business now, Harry. And my work is demanding... not much time for fashion these days." Miranda was exhausted. She was glad to have a day off. She needed a long weekend.

Harry missed those times when he took her shopping, and she came home and tried on everything in her pretty shopping bags. She would twirl and spin until she became dizzy and fell into his lap, giggling and kissing him. Miranda missed him too, laughing with him, sleeping with him. She missed loving Harry...

"Harry..." She was going to ask him where he was. Maybe they could go have dinner someplace.

He interrupted. "I was just thinking about how much you've changed." He was proud of her. "So. What exactly are you doing in your dining room?"

"I just painted it red!" She sounded like a girl again—*his girl.*

"That sounds great! Are you actually going to *eat in there?* Have you taken up *cooking...* or have you found a restaurant that caters our favorite fillet mignon sandwiches?" He was thinking about the home they once shared. She desperately wanted a Jenn-Air—pleaded with him— then used the oven to store her dictionary, thesaurus, and a stack of notebooks. She never cooked a meal; Harry loved her anyway. Miranda was always a much better writer than a chef. He cleared his throat, a crack in his smile.

"Is it like our dining room at home?"

"Brighter, shinier, but yes... sort of like that."

"I bet it's beautiful, Miranda, just like..."

"It is. Where are you?"

"I just left home and I'm heading to Mallard Point for the weekend."

Mallard Point? Why was he going there? They always had such a great time on their boat, but that's before Charlie Fine seduced her and ruined everything. Why didn't she sense he was a pirate, the worst of his kind?! She had an adoring husband and a happy life. Miranda took a deep breath. She could sense the conversation going downhill.

"Oh... so you're still a member?"

"I had no reason to leave, Hun... I wasn't the one who caused all the commotion. And in case you're wondering, Charlie Fine is still a member, too... shows no remorse." She recognized his icy tone.

"Are you by yourself?" Maybe she could drive to Traverse City and meet him...

"Mandy is coming up to join me later. She had a doctor's appointment, just a routine ultrasound."

"Who? A girl with a baby? What are you talking about?"

"I got married, Miranda. Mandy is having our baby."

Miranda felt a knife graze her skin, familiar droplets of crimson and wine seeping through a T-shirt already stained with red paint. There was a loud crack as the blade crashed through her rib cage and into her heart.

She asked again in a louder tone, "What are you talking about? We both know that's not possible! How in the world did you make a baby? And how could you do it without *me*?"

"Medical science has come a long way since you and I went to the doctor to find out if we could have a child. You remember that, right? I know you were pretty upset."

"Do I remember? Harry, it was my birthday... the day I found out we would never have a family!! I was so depressed I started drinking every night! *Do I remember!?* Yeah, I'm pretty sure I do!"

"I didn't mean to upset you."

"Did you get married the day after you were on my boat? The day you asked me to come home?"

"We had been seeing each other... "

"And she got pregnant."

"Something like that."

Miranda felt another prick against her skin, a surge, more blood. The sensation was painless compared to her suffering. Coughing, choking, it was getting hard to breathe. "Harry, how could you do this to me!? That's my baby! A girl named 'Mandy' is having my baby!" Miranda did the math, thought about Mandy, seven months along, a scary apparition with a big belly, fangs, and big dirty feet. She sounded gross.

It was just like that Barry Manilow song, "Mandy." Everyone in her class at school hated that song. *"Oh, Mandy.... well you came and you gave without taking... but I sent you away, awe Mandy."* Some people even said that song was about a *horse!* Can you believe it— a friggin' *HORSE!?* Harry should send her away, just like in the song. Miranda knew him all too well... he would never be happy with a pregnant girl named Mandy.

She had completely snapped.

"Miranda... Hun... I shouldn't have said anything. I didn't mean to upset you."

Miranda felt faint. She was seeing stars... like an old person who forgot to take their blood pressure pills then stands up too fast. She imagined Harry's new wife sitting in her old office at Stowe Publishing, scribbling on her Vera Bradley desk blotter with a crayon, a big ugly trench coat on the hook behind the door. The thought of it made her sick! She heard somebody calling her name...

"Miranda! Miranda! Listen. We can talk about this another time... sometime when you're feeling better." He worried about what she was going to do next. He'd seen her this way before, didn't know how she could handle a full-blown manic episode all alone. "Are you taking your medication? You said you were going to cut back on your drinking. You doing okay with that?"

If she drove out to Tommy's Gotcha for a drink and got in an accident he would never forgive himself. Traffic would be especially bad on a holiday weekend... reckless drunks would be everywhere. Miranda didn't mention that she had been sober since she started her job. What did it matter now anyway?

Miranda said, "I have to go."

"Is there anything I can do?"

A long pause...

"Don't ever call me. And don't call me Hun."

Miranda reached into a kitchen cupboard and took out an open bottle of vodka that she kept on hand for guests. She took half a Xanax to help her relax. Then she took the other half just to be sure. A drink would soften the blow about Harry. She climbed into bed, pulled up the covers, and slept till morning. With a migraine and a raging hangover, she was too sick to cry, and disappointed she would have to live another day.

Miranda wondered what terrible things she might have said to Harry. She held onto the wall and went downstairs to put on some coffee. Through squinting eyes, she opened the front door just enough to reach out with one hand and grab the newspaper, avoiding shards of sunlight that would make her head hurt worse. She poured a cup of coffee, sat down in her red dining room, and saw the headline.

"Traverse City Police have arrested a 22-year-old man on drunk driving and manslaughter charges in a crash that killed publishing magnate Harry Stowe and his wife Mandy Boyer Stowe, who was pregnant with the couple's first child. Police said the driver, Ricky Dodge of East Jordan, was driving north on Mallard Point Road and crossed into the opposite lane where the road narrows at the split, striking Stowe's Porsche 911 Carrera head on. Evidence obtained by the Michigan State Highway Patrol at the scene showed that Dodge was under the influence of alcohol. According to police, Mandy and Harry Stowe were pronounced dead at the scene."

Miranda passed out on the drop cloth, all spattered with red.

Seeking Miranda

Castle Rouge

Author's note: *A bipolar manic episode is bad. A bipolar mixed state is worse. The loss of Harry Stowe combined with an already unstable mood, set the stage for a devastating condition that combines the worst symptoms of both mania and depression occurring simultaneously. Impulsiveness, poor judgment, and suicidal ideation characterize a mixed state. Morbid thoughts, pressured speech, and substance abuse also can occur. Miranda is sick, so please don't judge her for what happens next.*

Emerson James Tiller hurt deeply for Miranda. She was more than just another employee working her way through the ranks of his company. She was curious and teachable, a quick study who could now manage any project. She was funny, and warm, and the clients loved her. Miranda represented Special Services with professionalism and class. Other than the day of her job interview, she never mentioned Harry Stowe, but he knew her well enough that behind her tough facade, she was devastated.

Tiller said she should take as much time as she needed, take on less responsibility, or maybe work closer to home for a while— anything that would help her through her grief. But Miranda wanted to get away, away from her little house where she last heard Harry's voice, Harry's smile. She wanted to be a safe distance from the office (and Neil Lipman) where no one would see her crumble. Tiller didn't know she was an alcoholic, about the chaos and trouble that followed her when she drank. It was critical that Tiller never saw her real, damaged self. She thanked him for his kindness and asked for her next project.

Miranda was assigned to a simple security installation at a downtown Detroit law firm. Her hopes of being with Harry again were gone, stolen by a drunk driver on Mallard Point Road. She wished the imaginary knives had been real, that she might have bled to death on the dining room floor. She reserved a suite at the Atheneum hotel, a place she stayed with Harry when they were in town. The staff was accommodating and discreet, and aside from an occasional meal from room service, Miranda would be left alone.

She loved the dramatic entrance to the lobby, the glass doors bordered by imposing Greek gods created in life-size stone relief. But this time the statues fueled her gloom. Miranda felt them looking down at her, their heads nodding in judgment. *How dare they condemn me? The accident wasn't even my fault! Fuck you!!* Were those thoughts in her head, or did she just say that out loud? She couldn't be sure. It had been a long day of travel. She was agitated and worn out. Miranda needed some rest, that's all. She would take her medication and feel better the next day.

Even though she was exhausted, Miranda couldn't fall asleep. She stayed awake most of the night, and got an early start with her crew in the morning. She was becoming the person she wanted to be— a hard working professional with a job to do. Her reputation mattered. The lawyers at the firm were bright and flirtatious, speaking in double entendres as she passed by.

Miranda wore her favorite Christian Louboutins that she got in Palm Beach... shiny five-inch stilettos with a trademark lacquer sole— perfect for everyday, certainly nothing outrageous. Whatever they were staring at, she let their comments slide. In spite of her grief, their attention made her feel good. When they invited her to join them for lunch, she accepted. It was Friday and the project had finished on schedule. It should have been her last day in the city. The group was seated at a long table. The lawyers ordered martinis, Miranda drank iced tea.

"I was thinking about going to the club tonight. Anyone in?" Mitchell was the attorney who was her go-to person at the job site. Beside him, a skinny young intern's ears perked up. He was eager to fit in with the cool kids.

"Yeah... that was a lot of fun last weekend, Mitch... *an interesting crowd."* He glanced at Miranda and snapped his striped suspenders.

"What about you, Miranda?" Their heads turned to look at her all at once. "You'll go to the club for a drink or two, won't you?" Miranda remembered the fun she had at the club with Harry. Their weekends at Mallard Point seemed like a million years ago. She considered their offer, thought it would be good to get out.

"I'll try anything once," she teased, acting bored with their childish plans. "Tell me where and when." No one knew she was under the spell of the most dangerous bipolar condition of all. Had they known, would it have mattered? Mitchell took the last bite of his steak sandwich, looked back at his friends, and winked.

That evening, Miranda sat alone at the hotel bar and ordered a scotch. It brought a warm, familiar rush that begged for more. She always had a drink when she was here with Harry, and it always turned out fine. So she had another. She handed the waiter a credit card, left a tip, and zipped shut her Prada Runway Bowler Bag, the one with real leopard print calfskin, made in New Zealand. Legend had it that it sold out in one day! Can you imagine? Though no longer a society girl, Miranda still liked to make the right impression. She wasn't sure exactly where she was going, but she knew Detroit could be a dangerous place— she needed to be careful.

Miranda breezed through the marble lobby, her tall shoes click-clicking with attitude. She cussed out the Greek gods as she passed through the glass doors onto the sidewalk. She asked the doorman to hail her a cab and told him the address. He seemed concerned, asked if she was sure. Miranda ignored his concern, got in the cab, and told the driver to take her there.

When she arrived at her destination, the driver said, "Are you *sure* this is where you want to be, Miss? Maybe I'll wait out here for just a minute, no charge, in case you change your mind." He was an older man with an Irish accent. Miranda dismissed his kindness, paid him, and waved him on.

Those two drinks at the hotel must have been really strong. And with that, she lost her balance, tripped over the curb, and stepped out of one of her shoes. "Damn," she mumbled... a huge scratch in her favorite red bottoms, a $1200 mistake. A man in a long, hooded cloak caught her before she hit the ground. *How odd,* she thought. His face was completely covered. Normally, this would have troubled her. That kind of contact with a stranger was way out of her comfort zone, but the scotch reassured her that he could be trusted. Miranda's troubled mind, Harry's fatal crash, and her declining sense of judgment would be her downfall. She heard the voice of mania hissing, beckoning her to go inside.

Meanwhile back in Petoskey, Drew Becker stood on the sidewalk in front of Miranda's little house, with a large pizza and a bag of Oreos. He wondered why the place was so dark. Of course, it was late, and maybe she was tired, but their Friday night pizza date had become something they both looked forward to. Miranda had just picked up six dining room chairs at an antique store in Alanson... European antiques so beautiful, it was worth stripping them down to the bare wood and starting over. It was supposed to rain all weekend. He figured they'd come up with a plan tonight, and in the morning get started. He drove his truck so there'd be plenty of room to run out and pick up supplies.

Drew got out his key, let himself in, and turned on the kitchen light. He knew she was working in Detroit, but she would have told him if she had to stay through the weekend. Drew was starving. With a slice of pizza in one hand, he took a beer from the fridge and sat down at the table to think. Two things stood out right away. One, the light on her answering machine was blinking, and two, her orchids on the kitchen windowsill were almost dead. These observations were equally disturbing. Drew wondered if she was drinking again.

He tried to be there for her when Harry died, but Miranda grew distant and cold, isolating herself as if they hardly knew each other. It's not like they were dating or anything, at least not in an official way. Even so, the big "kiss scene" on the dock at the Boat Basin had become legendary. He and Miranda had become local celebrities, and Kelly was the brunt of a growing repertoire of jokes for letting it happen. Poor Kelly.

Drew took another bite, turned on the light in Miranda's red dining room. It was a mess! There were old newspapers, half-eaten Eggo waffles, laundry not folded, and a pile of unopened mail. This was way out of character— something was wrong! He wasn't entirely comfortable being in her house alone. While they had become best friends and had a lot of fun together, he had only been in her bedroom once, and that was to break the seal on a window that had been painted shut. He turned on lights as he went through the house, noticing empty liquor bottles everywhere. His long legs climbed the stairs two at a time, and when he reached the top, he was shocked by what he saw.

For all her bragging about her huge walk-in closet and all her beautiful things, the second floor of the bungalow looked like a crime scene. Clothes were tossed on the floor, even her good suits for work were off the hangers and wrinkled. Her expensive handbags were carelessly thrown over a chair, their tissue paper stuffing strewn about. Drawers were carelessly left open. Her good lace bras and panties were unfolded in a laundry basket on the dresser. Drew never thought a tomboy like Miranda would wear underwear like that! He imagined her with him at the boathouse, curled up beside him on the old leather couch watching baseball, and wearing the sheer white bra and panties he held in his hand. In his fantasy she was a playful kitten, blond hair in a tangled mess, growling at him. He was getting distracted— now was not the time.

What Drew did next might mean the end of their friendship. But once, while she was getting settled in the house, he went to use the bathroom and saw pills— a lot of prescription bottles in the medicine cabinet. Drew was more than a master mechanic. He was good at computers, and quickly found out what the drugs were for. Miranda was unstable! She had bipolar disorder! Wherever she was, she could be in great danger!! He took one last look at the pretty things on the dresser, stored that image in his memory to be enjoyed at a later time, then ran back downstairs. He listened to the message on the machine and wrote the number on the back of his hand. He had no idea where she might be.

Miranda stood on the sidewalk in front of the dark and curious place. The man in the long, hooded cloak bent over and picked up Miranda's shoe, polished it on his sleeve, then placed it back on her pretty foot. He slipped away so silently she wondered if he was real. To the east, she saw fire in the distance, the flaming stacks of the Ford River Rouge plant. The plumes rose high above the Detroit River and lit up the sky like demons in flight. She watched as the silhouettes of tired workers walked to and fro, their loads of iron, limestone, and coal feeding the furnaces, their fat bellies gorging in the night. Even though the towers had not been active in years, the hallucination seemed very real. It was trying to seduce her.

The furnace throats screamed with laughter, sending their flames even higher. She stood at the entrance to Castle Rouge, a place far more daunting than the lawyers let on. The portico, of sorts, was a remnant from an ancient warehouse abandoned long ago, the door of steel painted red with no window. The building was bordered by empty row houses along a dusty road, the kind of neighborhood where if someone screamed, no one would hear. The thought of it fueled the heat that was building inside her.

Miranda's judgment smoldered in the ashes; a dog barked in the distance. On the sidewalk a man on a leash approached on all fours. He wore a rubber mask in the likeness of Bill Clinton and nothing else. An attractive woman with raven hair held the other end. The couple seemed at ease with their shocking appearance. The female opened the door, admonishing her pet to wait behind her. Miranda took a deep breath, a foolish chance, and followed them inside. Even in the dark, already drunk, she found her way to the crowded bar and made eye contact with a stranger. She smiled a demure smile and accepted his offer to buy her a drink.

Miranda might have prayed, that might have helped. The Palace Priests certainly would not want to see her at a place like this! But manic people don't do that— they don't pray, they don't ask for help, and they don't want to be told that what they're doing is wrong, dangerous, or even deadly! By now, Miranda's charm was irrepressible, her thoughts expansive and bold. She was glad to have a captive audience.

After checking her lipstick, she got up from the bar and stood a little taller in her shiny black shoes. She flashed her stilettos with prowess to anyone who might be her rival. So far, she had escaped hospitalization for her illness, and she wasn't about to turn herself in now— not to God, not her doctors, or Harry, or Drew, or Tiller! This was her big moment— *can't they see?!* What she did was none of their business. She left her phone at the hotel, just to be sure. With her glass empty, the fever of Castle Rouge in all its darkness took her away. The man on the leash drank beer from a water bowl. His mistress smiled, winked, and handed Miranda another drink.

Drew's Road Trip

Drew ran through the living room and into the kitchen, ignoring the half-eaten pizza. He stared at the answering machine, took a deep breath, pressed play, and wrote the number on the back of his hand. He flew out the door, jumped in his truck, and dialed the number. A man's voice answered, "This is Jim Tiller." Drew was at least 300 miles from Detroit, north by northwest of the city. He checked the time, looked to make sure he had a full tank of gas... then wondered what condition she would be in when he found her.

Drew headed out Mitchel Street. The road leading from Petoskey to the highway was narrow and winding, one of the most dangerous in the county. Even though he knew these roads like the back of his hand, he was driving with a sense of urgency and needed to be careful. It would take an hour to reach Wolverine, where 58 crosses I-75. He turned on some music, then turned it off again.

Drew thought about how much he liked spending time with her. She was sweet, and pretty, but she was also a girl who could take care of herself. Rumor had it that one night at Deeny's a guy came on to her and put his hands where they didn't belong. She put down her pool cue, decked him, and went back to her game. She was probably drunk, but still. Miranda was a walking contradiction... but that's what made her interesting, at least to the man who loved her.

Drew turned on his brights, tapped the brakes, then started down a long hill with a hard right turn at the bottom, watching for deer along the tree line. He headed up the next hill, and laughed out loud when he thought about the name on her transom. Whoever heard of a boat name with diamonds and a red lipstick? No wonder her dockmates made fun of her! Even so, it had as much sparkle and shine as she did. And then there was the time he got to her house a little early on a Saturday morning. She answered the door wearing an extra-large Michigan State t-shirt, tube socks, and a small Papillon; not a dog, but one of her expensive (and not very attractive, as far as he was concerned) designer handbags. When Drew was first getting to know Miranda (and had yet to learn about her collection), he actually thought Louis Vuitton might be her ex-boyfriend.

He tapped the brakes and swerved to avoid hitting a possum. Drew was counting on the information he got from Jim Tiller to locate her once he reached the city. He passed an occasional house, a church, and a pine tree farm on the left. He wondered if they might be a couple someday, as unlikely as that might be, given her former lifestyle and his desire for simpler things. There was a lot about him she didn't know. Considering Miranda's condition and reckless past, it would be a long time before he could trust her to have that talk.

He slowed down coming into Wolverine, a well-known speed trap. It was a sad little town with three churches, six bars, and an ATM. He could not imagine why anyone would want to live there. At the corner he turned left, turned right, turned right, then turned left again. That annoying dogleg could be dangerous in the dark, but there was no time to waste complaining about it. He got on I-75 south and headed for Detroit.

Drew remembered when Miranda bought the house in Petoskey, how he rode his motorcycle up from Charlevoix almost every weekend. They ate their way through mountains of Oreos and watched their favorite Alfred Hitchcock movies over and over. *North by Northwest* was Miranda's favorite. She liked sitting close to him on the sofa, waiting for the scene where the speeding train disappears into the dark tunnel. She always grinned and glanced up at him, batting her eyes and looking so innocent. It was as suggestive and sexual as any scene in a modern film, and she wondered if he would ever take the hint when she teased him that way. Drew knew exactly what she was thinking, but would not acknowledge it. Why were they playing these cat and mouse games when they had never even been on a real date?

The Grayling exit was 16 miles ahead. Drew had been on the highway well over two hours and needed to top off his gas tank and grab a couple of sandwiches. Even in a crisis a man's gotta eat. Drew put on his turn signal, tapped the brakes, and followed the ramp down to the light. He was driving way too fast. He stopped at Honkers, a gas station mini mart where they have decent food, clean restrooms, and stuffed dead geese mounted on the ceiling. He was back on the road in ten minutes flat.

It was another three hours to Detroit. Drew didn't reminisce often; life was too complicated to keep looking back. But he was at peace with his simple life on the lake, and that was something to be happy about. When he inherited the old boathouse after his grandfather died, he knew he would stay there forever. Among his favorite memories were summer afternoons walking through town as a boy, watching Hank Becker shake hands and make conversation with charter captains, and flattering the pretty girls.

Drew remembered sitting quietly eating ice cream sandwiches from the drug store, and watching with amazement as his grandfather turned wrenches and brought crusty old motors back to life. As Drew grew older, the two became inseparable, fishing in the morning, fixing boats all day, and walking the docks together at night. When the old man died, Drew missed him terribly. It left a huge void in his heart. People said his grandfather was old, that he had had a good life. And that was true. But the loss still hurt. Everything Drew

Becker knew about life, boats, and women, he learned from old Hank.

People wondered why Drew Becker chose to follow in his grandfather's footsteps rather than going to work for his father, William Becker, in the family business. What started as a single tie-up dock for Hank's old Hacker, was developed and marketed by his parents as one of the finest luxury marinas in northern Michigan. Every year William Becker added more docks and services, a pool, a restaurant, and a bar— even a concierge desk to help members set up tee times and book ferry rides. Though many were impressed by his father's success, Drew had no interest in the commercial conquests that drove his parents. Every time he grabbed the keys off the hook by the door at the boathouse, a wave of nostalgia told him he had made the right choice.

He remembered living a life of privilege as a boy, and being paraded around the Little Harbor Club dressed in a navy blue blazer and khaki shorts. Otherwise, Drew was left with nannies so his parents could have drinks at five with their equally rich friends. For all the years his parents couldn't have children, Drew showed up quite by surprise later in life. He was their pride and joy, their proper yacht club trophy. Drew lost interest in the things his parents valued most, mainly the Bridge Street Marina, the jewel in his father's financial crown.

William Becker always imposed on his son the value of a good education and the importance of making money. He preached at him endlessly about the benefits money could provide— travel, high quality friends, luxury goods and services, and membership at the right places. Without their membership to the Little Harbor Club, they would have missed out on so many of the good things in life. The Beckers were a respected and successful family. His mother served on some of the most important local committees, and they socialized with the wealthiest couples in northern Michigan, including the Governor. *That's what money can buy*, he would tell his son.

Yes, William Becker made millions, but Drew sometimes questioned how he got so much money in the first place. Even the most successful marina in Michigan is only seasonal, and could never generate the kind of money his father was worth. So Drew worked on boats by day, watched sports and wrote poetry by night. His parents stopped trying to control him, and Drew didn't miss their interest in running his life. When his parents died, he had regrets about all the years they were estranged, but that was Drew's cross to bear— the alternative may have been worse. Despite the leather jacket, rough hands, and a motorcycle, he was a sensitive and caring guy. But for now, his only concern was his friend.

Miranda's eyes had adjusted to the dark. It wasn't the alcohol, or the cab ride, or the Greek gods in the lobby that called Miranda away that night. It was her own desire that took her to Castle Rouge, a simultaneous race for pleasure and pain, an adventure deep into the secret places no one should go. The bipolar episode that was cast upon her like a spell left her helpless against temptation, and behavior that otherwise may not have suited her. *Or would it?* Miranda was too detached from her world to fear its outcome— her shiny things no longer mattered. All the money, and furs, and diamonds that fed her appetite shattered like glass at her feet, her pretty Louboutins ruined forever. Miranda finished her drink and took her first real look around Castle Rouge. This would be the most disturbing part of her journey.

She spotted a tall man wearing a black vest, no shirt, and leather motorcycle gloves. In a way he looked like Drew— or was it her troubled mind wishing he was there beside her, protecting her from the dark? She looked at the man for a moment, but couldn't be sure. Somewhere a cage door slammed shut... she heard a girl scream! The voice was familiar. Was it her own? Was she imprisoned? Some sort of trouble? She watched as a man dressed like a pirate with a shiny steel hook walked past, his date, much younger and very pretty was his wench. Her feathered mask covered her in a way her velvet bustier did not. *It was Charlie Fine! The pirate who stole her away! But was it?* His unmistakable wiry red hair was missing, and his eyes never met her own. Perhaps she was mistaken...

Miranda was seeing colors where there were none; a hallucination of sparkle and fizz that excited her! She looked through the faces and costumes of the crowd and past an imaginary horizon. It was cold. She let the wind carry her back to Tommy's Gotcha to visit the men she once knew there. Her sense of clarity surpassed all the drinks she had consumed, or so she believed. The vision came to life as she got closer. Miranda scanned the faces on the barstools and discovered that her old friends were really pirates, too—strangers to be shunned, evil dancing all around them! She could see it so clearly now! How could she not have known!?

Harry Stowe, (who was of course not drinking), sat at the end of the bar, his eyes glued to the current issue of *Car and Driver.* The Porsche on the cover appeared to be his own, the one from the crash that killed him. His pirate shirt was clean and pressed, handsome as ever. He glanced up at her, a look of disappointment on his face. *But how could that be? Was he real?* He sat beside his nemesis, Charlie Fine, who was already undressing her with his golden, wolf-like eyes... a cigarette dangling from the corner of his mouth. Miranda breathed in his smoke and felt strangely aroused. She could never escape Charlie's magic.

There was Vince the cowboy, his sidekick Buster, and Neil Lipman who was playing with his own tiny sword. Joe Ramono looked at his watch, always concerned about the time. It was almost midnight. The group looked ridiculous in their pirate hats and ruffled blouses. But even dressed in costumes of frivolity, each wore an expression that was serious. This was no party! They raised their glasses in a toast, saluting each other for keeping Miranda from the truth all these years. She squinted her eyes and watched as matching gold signet rings, just like Charlie's, were revealed on each man's hand, shining bright enough to blind her even in the dark. Even Harry Stowe wore the ring, which seemed unlikely since jewelry could easily scratch his car. None of this made any sense!

One of the pirates said her name, she recognized the voice. He was the most colorful of all the characters, a dashing Pirate King! Tastefully turned out for the occasion, he wore a velvet hat with a huge ostrich plume, ornate gold braiding all around, and a Florida tan even though it was out of season. His silver hook, unlike Charlie's, was lying flaccid atop the bar. Even without his navy blue blazer, Miranda recognized the mysterious man with the silver ponytail and piercing blue eyes. He said her name again, and motioned for her to join him.

With a flourish, he waved his arm directing her eyes to the treasure all around him. He grinned and evil grin, tipped his hat, and handed her something. Miranda felt a chill, and wondered if she was seeing things. But the gold bar in her hand was real. She ran from the scene, noting the absence of her three dockmates and a seventy year old man named Tommy. Jim Tiller stood erect by a tall stone archway. Dressed in a dark suit, leather gloves and dark glasses, she knew he was there to protect her. The pirates roared with laughter as she stumbled back into reality, back into the darkness of Castle Rouge.

She heard the cage door again, closer now. Another scream! Was someone hurting her? *Was that her own voice?* She wondered, but couldn't be sure. She was getting sleepy. The pirates made her afraid. They ruined everything! She would drink a lot of water to dilute the alcohol. That always helped. *Honestly... I feel fine.* She saw two girls kissing, the pirates gathering to watch.

There is no escaping, Miranda... stay here... join in the fun. The Castle whispered her name in a voice that was deep and foreboding. A strong, cold arm reached out and pulled her close. *What are you drinking? Can I get you another? This is the right place for you, Miranda... come to the party and play with me..."*

The words calmed the mania raging inside her. It gave her peace, like a prayer. Perhaps the voice was someone who could help her... or maybe Castle Rouge was calling, eager to show a beginner the way. The faceless man in the long black cloak nodded in agreement, so Miranda stayed. With a frigid burst of wind, her black dress magically transformed into a soft leather sheathe. It was cut low and fit tight against her skin. She had joined the costume ball!!

But I'm so tired... just need to sit down... no really, I'm fine. As Miranda began her descent, droplets of crimson and wine fell to the floor. She recognized a light spritz of Chanel No. 5. The pretty one from the painting reached through the cage and touched Miranda's soft cheek. Her small waist and shapely breasts made her more desirable than the girls around her. She took Miranda's hand, beckoning her to come close. A door opened. Miranda lowered her eyes, feeling unsure but willing. Pirates were everywhere, watching, waiting, and panting like dogs. She wondered if the girl in the painting was really her.

Seeking Miranda

Carousel

Life is special
life is fun
see Miranda
on the run
shooting pool
in bars at night
sees a hussy
picks a fight.

Taverns give her
drinks for free
keep her there
and you will see
the pirates gather
circling near
drunk Miranda
has no fear.

Lips of ruby
brush the glass
drinking whiskey
warms her fast.
Judgment drifting
shifting sands
draw her into
pirate hands.
"Pour another round,"
says he,
"and come back to
my ship with me."

An angry God
a frosty glance
to honor him
she stands no chance.
When morning comes
with bleary eyes
she cries alone
her choice unwise.

The carousel goes
round and round
her pirate world
is going down
faster than the
drink she craves
by 5 o'clock
she finds her way

beyond another
place of shame
Miranda's here
let's play the game.

Can such a girl
reclaim her youth?
an orchid fades
belies the truth
and turns to face
the pages past
but time is gone
the spell's been cast.

Gangplank waiting
spirit bound
true forgiveness
nowhere found
her lonely nights
in all despair
she hopes that God
is waiting there.

Now I lay me
down to sleep
if God is real
I hope he'll keep
his eyes on me
all thru the night

where evil reigns
and dark is light

The Paramedics

The man standing over her had a serious expression. The couch she was resting on felt familiar. Miranda recognized the squeeze of a blood pressure cuff and a stethoscope pressed to her chest. She saw an IV bag hanging over her, but felt nothing. "Miranda, can you tell me what day it is? Who is the president, Miranda, do you know? What year is this? Miranda, wake up! You have to stay awake now..."

Who was this man, and why was he shouting at her? She opened her eyes again. The light in the window was blinding. It was giving her a headache. She squinted and saw her dining room, red as ever. *She was at home?* Then, another surge in her gut, face wet with sweat and grime, and whatever else her sordid adventure had left behind. More dry heaves. She wondered if she was dying. From the look of her dress, she had vomited—vomited a lot.

As sick as she was, she noticed that someone had the good sense to put a sheet on her expensive leather couch. Three paramedics in matching shirts hovered over her, checking her vital signs. One reported that her respirations were back in the normal range, and her temperature was steadily improving. Drew was exhausted from the ordeal. He was still puzzled. *What was she even doing at a place like that?* Evidently, there were still certain parts of her life she needed to keep secret, even from him.

Miranda tried to take a deep breath, wondering if the oxygen mask would hide her tears. She wondered who found her. If Drew picked her up at Castle Rouge, she could never face him again. When she went there that night, she had no idea it was that kind of place. That must be what the cab driver meant when he said he wanted to wait for her in case she changed her mind. Now she wished she would have listened.

Worse yet, Miranda wondered how Tiller found out. There was no way he could have known unless someone at the law firm ratted her out. Miranda was always very careful to cover her tracks when she was drinking. She always did an impeccable job of concealing certain things about her life— not lying, exactly— *just protecting.* She could not figure out where she went wrong this time. Miranda tried to speak, coughed, and pulled off the oxygen mask. "How long was I gone?" The pain in her stomach twisted and pulled... she heard herself moan.

"We can talk about that later," said Drew in a calming tone. He squeezed her hand. "The most important thing now is to make sure you get plenty of rest and give your body a chance to recover." Miranda didn't want to talk about it later. In fact, she wasn't going to talk about it, period! *People needed to stay out of her business!* She was still drunk enough to believe she was making sense.

If she wanted to stop drinking, she could quit any time. Any day!! What makes people think they have the right to judge her? Even the Bible says you're not supposed to do that! If Drew or anyone else wanted to know what goes on at a place like that, they can rent a video, ha ha. That would certainly shake things up!

"I'll stay with you till you're better, or at least until they get the test results." *What was Drew talking about? It was a bar! There were not any tests!* "The police said they've had problems with date rape drugs lately. It's better to know for sure..." *Oh, this was all so bad... so, so bad. She could think about it later. How could this have happened?*

"She's dehydrated from all the diarrhea and vomiting," said the paramedic in charge. "She's stable for now. Her vitals are almost normal. She will be fine as long as you keep an eye on her, get her to drink plenty of fluids. If she shows any signs of having a seizure, get her to the ER right away."

"Alcohol poisoning can be pretty bad, sometimes even fatal," said the one with the stethoscope. Evidently, Miranda collapsed when she got out of Drew's truck, insisting she didn't need his help. When he couldn't get her to talk to him, he acted quickly, called EMS. He was glad he drove to Detroit to find her, glad he called Tiller to help track her down. He was, however, getting tired of trying to help someone who refused to help herself.

The paramedic in charge checked her heart rate one last time and made a note that the color had returned to her face— wonderful news for those who wanted her alive, a disappointment for those who would prefer otherwise. Even though she was still buried in a queasy drunken fog, she knew the carnage would be vast. And as for Jim Tiller, she couldn't even bear to think about the damage she'd done. Miranda wondered about her Bible, the one she used to read on her boat. She said a quiet prayer and asked God to take away her hangover, fix the damage she did to her friendship with Drew, and make Tiller forget everything that happened that night.

"When you ask, you do not receive, because you ask with wrong motives, that you may spend what you get on your pleasures." James 4:3

Miranda was soaking in the tub contemplating the rest of her life and reading about the side effects of her new medication. She believed if God was real, he would answer her prayer and everything would be okay— and the sooner the better. She was listening to her favorite recording of Brahms Sonata for Cello and Piano # 2 in F, which always soothed, her until now.

Headache. Agitation. Nausea. Vomiting. Did she really want to take pills that made her feel worse instead of better? Insomnia. Weight gain. Drooling. Acne. The minute she gained one pound she was through. Even though she didn't think her recent bipolar episode was all that bad, her doctor thought otherwise and prescribed more drugs. Miranda was certain he was overreacting. Anxiety. Vertigo. Suicidal thoughts. Priapism. (She looked it up. It only happened to men. And this was a bad thing?) And oh, yes, under certain circumstances this medication will kill you.

She slid down into the water, admiring her red painted toenails through a mountain of Mr. Bubble. While the alcohol-related nausea and vomiting had finally passed, she had mixed feelings about any medication that was almost guaranteed to make her look bad and feel worse— not especially appealing on a job interview, a date, or otherwise.

It had been almost two weeks since Drew brought her home from Detroit— sick, severed, and broken. He stayed a few days, encouraged her, held her hand, and brought her endless bottles of Gatorade, just as the paramedic ordered. But in spite of her feelings for him, Miranda just wanted him to go home. She appreciated his concern, but when alcoholics are backed into a corner or confronted with their behavior, they isolate. That's just the way it is, and that's what she wanted to do.

The water had turned cold. Miranda stepped out of the tub and wrapped herself in a fluffy white towel. The face in the mirror was so pale and thin, and her eyes were rimmed with dark circles. No wonder Drew was worried. For the first time she was starting to see how her drinking was taking its toll. She looked older than her years and feared that no amount of vanity or magic potions could repair the damage. Even though she dreaded facing the world in her current state of disrepair, she knew she would have to find a job.

While it hurt Tiller to let her go, she understood company policy and the documents she signed the day she was hired. The nature of her work called for exemplary behavior on the job and off. Miranda represented *Special Services* and she had done it poorly. Even though she was sure her boss knew about her binge, (Tiller was omnipresent, nothing got past him), she felt his sadness when he shook her hand and patted her shoulder goodbye. She choked back tears, knowing how much she would miss him and the work she did with his firm. She was very alone.

She pulled on a t-shirt, put on some red lipstick, and headed down the steps for the door. Losing her job was a devastating consequence of her bad behavior. But it was nothing compared to the aftermath that was yet to come.

Weed Eater

Courtesy Notice

This is a courtesy notice from the City of Petoskey, Michigan, to inform you that your grass has exceeded the maximum height of 8 inches established by City Ordinance Section 11-1996. Please comply within 7 days to avoid a $50 fine.

Sincerely,

James R. Lipman (no relation)
Petoskey City Manager

It was late on a rainy Monday when Miranda came home from the bars. On her way in she noticed a catalog, soaking wet on her porch— *Nordstrom Fall Collection,* great clothes, very expensive, very depressing. She had avoided her mailbox for days, knowing that there would be lots of bills and only one unemployment check to cover them.

She dropped the pile on the dining room table, ate two stacks of Oreos, and flipped through the envelopes. That's when she spotted the official looking piece from the City. She opened it, read the notice, and decided it would still be there in the morning. She shuffled toward the stairs, kicked off her shoes, and slowly climbed her way to another drunken night's sleep.

The next day, fighting a migraine, she read the notice again. Miranda slipped on big dark glasses, a hat, and a long silk robe. She grabbed a ruler from the kitchen drawer and indignantly marched out to the front yard— Greta Garbo meets the City of Petoskey. It was 9:00 a.m. and her neighbor, 80-year-old Eugenia Greene was already hard at work in her yellow kitchen apron, tending to her plants, and greeting the birds in song. The tulips, leaning and bending to an offshore breeze, were resplendent dressed in the colors of spring. Eugenia Greene was a vision of loveliness— Miranda was not. The grass was up to her knees and she was outraged.

"This is man's work... how dare they?!" she cried. The sight of her tall grass took her back to the days when a lawn and landscape crew tended to the grounds at the castle, while she sipped lemonade on the porch swing with Harry. Sometimes she wondered whatever happened to those guys, Brother John and Brother James, the men who encouraged Miranda to find a more spiritual way of life, one based on the love of God and the Bible, and not just the pursuit of more stuff. Given her current state of affairs, they were probably right. Life had become so hard. She wished she would have listened to them while she still had the chance, but she was too busy shopping. Sadly, those days were gone. Her grass was too long, and she didn't have 50-dollars to pay the city. She hated asking for help. Calling Drew to rescue her (again) was out of the question.

An hour later, exhausted and sweating through her cut-off shorts and Michigan State t-shirt, the lawn was mowed, and Miranda felt a huge sense of accomplishment, despite the grass stains on her good Coach sneakers. She returned the old mower to the shed, picked up the Black and Decker weed eater left by the former owners when she bought the house— Model ST1000— clean, hardly used.

With renewed confidence, she plugged in the cord, walked toward the fence that bordered the south side of her property, and flipped the switch. No sound. She was, after all, an experienced trouble shooter from her days aboard the old boat. A simple lawn tool was not going to get the best of her. She unplugged the unit and turned the ST1000 upside down to take a look. Miranda pushed on the string cartridge, heard a click, and stood still in her tracks as the twine released itself, encasing her with an angry snap.

Eugenia Greene turned away from her work to see Miranda wildly flinging her arms this way and that, only making her confinement worse. She called across the yard, "Need a hand, Miss Miranda? I've threaded plenty of weed eaters in my day. I'll just grab my pruning shears so we can cut you out of that mess." Miranda, still flailing, was fuming. Her life had taken a dreadful turn for the worse, and this was the last straw! She was a prisoner of her own making, a Black and Decker captive, a fool in her own front yard.

She remembered a paper with a list of motivational sayings that Drew had taped to her refrigerator. There was one that said, *if you don't like it, change it!* He told her the quotes were filled with wisdom and sometimes inspired his poetry. And that gave Miranda an idea. "No thanks, Mrs. Greene. I will not be needing any advice or help with weed eaters ever again. In fact, this is the last time you will see me out here mowing, trimming, or otherwise." Eugenia Greene put down her pruning shears and cocked her head, wondering if she heard right. "From now on I will be devoting my time to something worthwhile, something I'm actually quite good at. I am going out to find a rich husband so I can live in a house with landscapers to do all the work, *so I won't have to!*

Miranda brushed herself off and headed straight for the kitchen. There was a recipe box in the pantry under the stairs. She took it from the shelf, looked inside, and held it close to her heart. She breathed a sigh of relief, poured a tall glass of Gatorade, and carried the box to the dining room. Without wasting a minute, she emptied the box and spread the contents around on the table, a puzzle waiting to be solved. She turned over the cards and arranged them in neat columns and rows. Some were special and brought back nice memories, while others she couldn't remember at all. She sifted through the business cards and saw there was hope. Where Miranda's lawn and landscape nightmare ended, a new world of possibilities began.

Of course, there were no recipes in the box— this adventure was not about cooking! Miranda picked up a card, and read it out loud.

Kenneth Mann
Maple Point Amusement Park
Landscape Architect

She picked up another.

Russell Taylor
American Airlines
Senior Captain

She recalled that he was impossibly handsome and wore a Breitling Bentley... one of the most expensive watches of all time. She slid his card to the right, away from the others.

The next one...

Martin Sheets
Sheets Memorials and Monuments
Family owned since 1968

He handed her his card one night at Jack's Steakhouse while Miranda was living aboard at the Boat Basin. Even though she did not actually remember him, she recalled that he lived on the peninsula at Bay Harbor. He was single, successful, and also had a place on Mackinaw Island. She placed his card next to Captain Taylor.

There must have been 100 business cards in front of her, all from men she'd met along the way, some on jobs with Tiller, others in bars at night. They'd say things like, "Call me sometime when you're in town," or "Maybe we can have lunch." She was enjoying a walk down memory lane. At last, the pieces of her shattered life were starting to fall into place! She would arrange the cards in priority order, choose the top 30, then go on a date with each one— 30 dates in 30 days! This would provide a nice variety of men for her to meet, and when all the dates were finished, she would pick the best one to be her husband. Everything was going to be alright.

Miranda heard the sound of Drew's truck in her driveway. This always meant something good was about to happen. She was still seated at the table when Drew let himself in. He had a bag of Chinese carry out, a coconut cream pie, and a bag of Cheetos for later. He leaned over, kissed her neck, and went into the kitchen for some plates. Miranda got goosebumps and shivered. Was it the General Tsao's Chicken? Or the way his skin smelled on a hot day? They had patched things up as much as possible. He accepted her most sincere apology, and there was no discussion about what went on that night in Detroit. She sat twirling her hair, listening to

Dvorak, and sipping Gatorade through a straw. She was extremely excited to see him. Drew studied her face. Something didn't look right.

By this time the cards were arranged into two neat piles— those that made the cut, and those that did not. There were still a few loose ends, but she was happy with her work so far. And she was starving, happy to take a break for some dinner. "So what are you workin' on over there, Kitten? Looks like a big project." More goosebumps. She melted like butter when he called her that. Why did carry out with Drew taste better than dinner at a five-star restaurant with anyone else? For all the years she spent married and trying so hard to be perfect, Miranda wondered why it was so easy to be with him when she was not.

"I'm guessing by the big ball of twine in the front yard that things didn't go so well earlier?" He wrapped his arms around her then stopped. She held up one finger gesturing for him to wait. Miranda was having a moment of clarity and needed to take one more look at the cards on the table.

"Do you recognize this one... a D.W. Manos? I don't recall ever meeting anyone by that name." She liked his business card. It was shiny.

Drew picked up the card. It was gold metallic on both sides, with his name and a P.O. Box in Miami, nothing more. Drew couldn't even imagine what kind of person would have a business card like that. It was strangely familiar. He imagined someone who wore a gold pinky ring and drank martinis— not exactly a man's man. He looked back at the mess on the table. "Miranda, what is all this stuff? What's going on here?"

"You can pitch all of these if you want," she said, handing him the cards that she rejected.

Drew liked Miranda more than he let on. He liked that she was smart, and funny, and was intrigued by her wild side—something the guests at Castle Rouge might have seen that night, but something he clearly had not. There was no physical relationship between them. She had not shown much interest in taking their friendship to the next level, and he wasn't sure exactly why. That kiss on the dock last spring was a prank, he understood that. Frankly, he didn't like Kelly either, and was happy to oblige. But Drew was a gentleman and would never push himself on a girl.

She pretended to be one of the guys, and considering the way she handled herself during the big storm, she certainly had everyone's respect. He was impressed when she said she changed her own oil— the twin 454's would intimidate most men. And while he wasn't sure how much of it was true, he would have given anything to have watched her handle the Ferretti. He liked that she was a tomboy. But in his imagination late at night, Drew thought about her in a different way.

She was tall and fit, a mix of strength and curves, beautiful but undone in a way that was so damn sexy. He thought about the way her shiny blond hair and red lipstick were perfect for work every day, but loved her most with her curls tucked inside a ball cap, or tumbling down in a windblown mess. He liked her best when she liked herself. He liked her least when she was drinking.

Drew wasn't sure what kind of mischief she was planning with all these business cards, but something seemed very wrong. Drew took her hands from the table, squeezed them tight in his own. "Why don't you take a break from your project. Let's have some dinner and you can tell me all about it."

Seeking Miranda

Thirty Dates

Miranda was ready to proceed with the next step of her plan. With a stack of Crane Stationary announcement cards (ecru with a gold embossed Fleur-des-lis at the top) she began the arduous task of letting her potential suitors know that she was available. A tasteful handwritten note canceled out the tackiness of inviting one's self on a date— or at least that's what she decided. Her calendar began to take shape, weekends filling up first, the rest of the days taken by older retired men and rich guys who didn't have to work.

First was an electrical engineer retired from General Electric with six patents pending. He prepared a wonderful spaghetti dinner aboard his sailboat, using his own invention to bake homemade bread in the microwave. He was leaving Petoskey soon to sail around the world. Miranda liked him, but there was no chemistry— she wasn't the science type.

The next contestant was an independently wealthy young man her own age, dressed in tight jeans and a Jhane Barnes shirt. In some ways, he was a dead ringer for Michelangelo's Statue of David. In other, more important ways, he was clearly not. He had recently returned from climbing Mt. Everest and was in Petoskey visiting his mother. While he was planning to leave soon for his home in San Diego, Miranda was taken by his charm, movie star looks, and other promising qualities. He moved up the list.

There was a fifty-ish chiropractor who lived in a house on the beach at L'Arbre Croche. He was fashionably turned out, and wearing a Christian Lacroix necktie that cost more than her first car. Miranda found herself attracted to him. But when he polished his silverware on the tablecloth before the salads arrived, all she could think of were Harry's boxer shorts, neatly pressed and on hangers. A second date she would have to decline.

A sexy dentist with a house on The Bluff was soft spoken and likable as dentists typically are— at least at first. The date ended quickly when he whispered something in Miranda's ear and sent her running. There would not be another night at Castle Rouge or any place like it in her future, no matter how much money he had. Another disappointment was a man who owned a chain of Hallmark stores throughout northern Michigan. Unlike the dentist, he was so thoughtful and sensitive that he could not stop quoting Maya Angelou. A little goes a long way.

Her favorite date so far was with a judge in the Court of Common Pleas, whose power to put people in jail she found enticing. He also turned out to be married—better to find that out sooner rather than later this time. After that, she went out with a retired FBI agent who was assigned to Washington D.C. during the Nixon administration. He had the best stories to tell, and wore a gun strapped to his ankle. A nice touch, Miranda made a note.

Next, she went out to dinner with a friend of a friend, trusting that her high standards in men would be upheld. They had dinner at an Italian restaurant in the middle of nowhere. He had the same last name as a notorious Detroit crime family, but then gave her a David Yurman bracelet as an ice breaker, which was a nice touch. After dinner he took $1000 cash from his wallet, and asked her to have sex with him in the men's room. Miranda mentioned that she was dating an FBI agent, a judge, and also that she was worth twice that. He scoffed at her comment then called her a cab. She had no interest in dating a mob boss, and she already had plenty of nice jewelry.

Miranda had dinner with an NHL hockey player from Detroit. While he was missing most of his teeth, the aggressive nature of the game made him strangely appealing, and his status as a professional athlete scored extra points in overtime. Oddly, her next date was with a network affiliate sportscaster who hated hockey, but promised Miranda free tickets and very good seats.

She went out with a cartoonist from the Free Press who was only funny on paper, an aerobics instructor who was openly gay but showed her a really nice time, and a bank president who wore a tattered plaid sport coat to their date at Bob Evans. Whether he was just cheap or broke, this would never do.

She dated the butcher, the baker, the candlestick maker... went out with doctors, lawyers, and Indian chiefs, not to mention every Tom, Dick, and Harry. But nothing so far really struck her fancy. Just before Date 29 she was made aware of a scheduling problem. A veterinarian from Ann Arbor, the owner of three tiny pugs, called to say that he was about to perform an emergency C-section on a prize-winning cow and would be tied up the rest of the week. Miranda remembered him well. While he wasn't as wealthy as most of her prospects, she probably liked him best. But hey, the show must go on.

She picked up her phone and dialed. "Drew... it's me."

"Hey, Kitten, what are you wearing?" There was a pause on the line, she smiled.

"Well let's see... I'm wearing shorts, my good sparkle flip-flops, and a sheer white T-shirt, somewhat clingy. Why do you ask?" (He always asked what she had on, and she loved flirting with him.) "Anyway, I know this is gonna sound crazy, but number 29 just cancelled... No, he had a legitimate excuse... Anyway, I was just wondering, and before you say no," (she could see him rolling his eyes). "Since we have never gone out on a real date, would you please take me to dinner tomorrow night? No alcohol, I promise. Okay, 7:00, can't wait."

Seeking Miranda

Drew and Miranda

After a nice dinner at Jack's Steakhouse, Drew invited Miranda to come back to the boathouse for dessert. It had been a wonderful first date, and Miranda did not want it to end. Drew hung his keys on a hook by the door, then reached in to turn on the light. The old stair planks creaked as they climbed up. A cool breeze tickled her bare legs as they reached the top. Lake Charlevoix was splashing and dancing in the dark below, begging to stay up late and play.

Drew kicked off his shoes and flopped down on the couch. He patted the spot beside him and turned on the TV. "C'mon and sit down, Kitten. It's only the top of the third... we can still catch most of the game. Can I get you something to drink? There's coconut cream pie in there... fresh cookies, too." Drew was a big sports fan and talked endlessly about how the Tigers were going to take the pennant this year.

Miranda was more interested in exploring where Drew lived. It was a small space, just two rooms, full of antique furniture and things gathered over time. "Feel free to look around, Kitten. You know, my grandfather built this place when he was my age. A lot of the stuff in here has been around forever." He returned from the kitchen with two glasses of milk and an unopened package of cookies. She sensed their first date was over, and now they would pick up where they left off, as playmates and friends— it was okay. Miranda had no expectations that it would ever be more.

She clasped her hands behind her back, her heels click clicking around the perimeter of the room. It was a sound that said, *I'm disappointed so I'll walk around and make noise until you pay attention to me.* She cleared her throat and stopped in front of the wall nearest the kitchen. Drew was going to ask her to get him another glass of milk, but decided this was not the time.

A proper oak bookcase displayed a collection of treasures from Drew's growing up years—an autographed baseball, a pine box derby car, some framed photos, and a pair of ticket stubs from a Van Halen concert.

There was a picture of Drew as a little boy standing on the dock with an old man, each of them holding one end of a big ugly fish. He was gloating; she knew the look. There was a faded black and white photo of an ancient canoe bottom boat, one of the first generation HackerCrafts. Several other pictures of woodies were displayed beside it.

Miranda leaned in and took a closer look at a photograph of a nice-looking couple in their late fifties, dressed in resort attire, and standing on the back deck of the Little Harbor Club. Knowing the cost of membership and annual dues, these people were loaded. Could they be his parents? And if so, why hadn't she seen them around? Some people were private that way. She didn't talk about her family, either.

On the center shelf there were pictures from Hessell. The annual boat show there, held every August, attracted the most beautifully restored and cherished vintage wood boats from all over the United States and Canada. Boats were trailered in from as far away as California and Florida. Drew once told her that his grandfather traded a man from Detroit a full boat restoration in exchange for one of the fancy new Hackers, the one with the modern V-hull that was built for speed. With a little work, that boat won best in show three years in a row. Tonight, it was covered up in the boathouse below, waiting for Drew to restore it when he had some spare time. Miranda had become a welcome distraction and so the boat would have to wait. Maybe Drew would invite her to go to Hessell with him someday...

Even when he was an old man, Drew's grandfather ran the boat all the way up Lake Michigan, east to the Mackinaw Bridge, and thirty miles northeast to the Les Cheneaux Islands. Drew always went with him. "He knew people everywhere we went... always took home a trophy. He knew the lakes like the back of his hand."

Drew was talking through a smile, and perhaps even some tears. She could see that his happiest moments growing up were when his grandfather was with him.

"Is the lady in this picture your grandmother?" Miranda was studying a small black and white photo that had faded with time. She could see the edges were cracked, as if it had been tucked inside someone's wallet for decades. It was an informal pose in front of an old train station. The woman was disheveled and lovely, holding onto Hank's arm. Drew hesitated. He wasn't prepared to talk about all this tonight. Someday he would tell her the whole story.

"It is," he said matter of factly.

"She's very pretty," Miranda noted. "What was her name?"

"Her name was Hattie. Someday I'll tell you all about her, but for now, why don't you come over here and sit down," he said in a mock serious tone. "Your milk won't stay cold forever."

She was a little put off that he'd rather watch baseball than entertain her. Even if nothing happened, she didn't want to have a face full of black cookie crumbs if it did. And besides, who knew what he was really thinking? Drew could be unpredictable that way. As she walked toward the sofa to presumably watch the game, she spotted an unusual end table next to an open window. It was covered by a crocheted doily with some magazines stacked on top. But before Miranda dismissed it as just another old piece of furniture, she spotted the faded monogram design, the distinctive trademark of legendary trunk maker, Louis Vuitton!

Her heart stopped. Her mouth went dry. She once told Drew she liked her handbags better than sex. She was mostly kidding, but still. "What's the story on this nice, old piece?" While she tried to sound calm, her hands were trembling and sweat was beginning to bead on her forehead.

It's been in that same spot for as long as I can remember. When I refinished the floors the year I moved in here, I just stained around it." Miranda laughed, secretly hoping no stain got on the trunk. It was worth a fortune. "If it wasn't so darn heavy, I'd have carried it out of here years ago." His voice got serious. "Why don't you come over here and sit down."

Miranda walked over to a worn leather couch. It was faded and scratched, maybe the favorite spot of a favorite dog at one time. She wondered about Hank Becker and his life at the boat house. Judging by the lines and creases crisscrossing the faded cushions, she wondered about the stories the old sofa might have to tell. Miranda sat down in a ladylike fashion, crossed her legs, and declined a cookie. He leaned over, took her face in his hands, and kissed her— *really kissed her.* "Kitten, you're shaking. Are you cold?... Nervous?... Or are you all worked up over that silly piece of luggage?" He liked to tease her.

He thought about the night he was alone in her house, the time he saw all those pretty, girlie things in her room. They were off limits that night— he was a gentleman, of course. But tonight, he was going to see them— *and see them on her.* Drew turned off the TV, closed the window, and lingered there for a moment. He glanced through the open door to his bedroom. The old quilt was plenty warm for him, but it was a cool night. Drew turned around and saw Miranda watching him. There was a knowing look on her face. They were going to be together at last... two friends that went on a date, all because Mr. 29 canceled.

"Miranda..."

"Hmmm?"

"I have more of those old trunks in my bedroom. Wanna see?"

Drew was not good at intimacy, but neither was she. He unzipped her dress; it fell to the floor. She turned around to face him. She was wearing a white lace bra and panties, the ones he saw in his dreams at night. She tilted her head and smiled. Drew had done all this before, there were plenty of girls in his past. But there was no one he wanted more. "Miranda. There aren't really any trunks in my room. I lied. Will you come to bed with me anyway?"

Maybe it was all the times they were curled up together on her couch, usually falling asleep before the movie was over. She knew him, trusted him. Miranda closed her eyes and focused all her attention on his big hands, the way they felt on her body, and the lace underwear he was tracing with his fingers. She thought about finally being upstairs at his boat house, about being in his bed after all this time. No other thoughts mattered... except one.

Miranda opened her eyes, giggled, then laughed out loud. Drew said, "You're thinking about the Hitchcock movie, aren't you..."

Miranda blinked twice and coyly replied, "No..." pretending she had no idea what he was talking about. She was incorrigible. He pinched her, she screamed.

"North by Northwest, Miranda... the part about the train. I knew what you were thinking the whole time...."

"Did not."

"Did, too."

She blushed. "Then tell me about the train then, Drew... was it coming?... or going? And if you know so much, then tell me... what were *you* thinking?" Even with her clothes off she was sassy, and clever, and had to have her own way. He laced his fingers through her hands and pushed them down against the mattress— she resisted. There would be plenty of time for her to be in control in the morning, but not now. She pulled hard to free herself, he tightened his grip and smiled...

"Drew..."

"Hmm..."

"Can I ask you something?"

"Of course, Kitten. What is it?"

She paused. "Nothing."

"What? *What?! Just tell me!"*

."I just wanted to know if... you know... I wondered if you... how you feel about me..."

"Miranda... you know I do... but that could all change if you *don't stop talking!!"*

He raised an eyebrow and winked at her.

She returned the look. He kissed her; she bit his neck. Miranda took a slow, deep breath of him. His skin was hot. She could feel herself sinking into the sheets with the weight of his strong body and broad chest on top of her. He tasted like sunshine, like the sky, like the open water on a summer day. She looked up at him, wanted him, and told him so. Drew saw a familiar, playful look in her eyes.

"Drew..."

"Hmm..."

"Tell me I'm your Kitten," she said in a whisper, as she arched her back, determined to free herself, and insisting he let her go! He ignored her and put his lips against hers, this time softer, slower than before, teasing her to kiss him back. She didn't have to perform for him, or flirt, or make the right impression. Maybe there were times like that in her past with other men, but things were different now.

Miranda felt strangely nervous, unsure of herself. She didn't like being out of control, and wasn't certain she should let her guard down, even with *him.* Drew brushed her cheek with his lips and whispered. "Relax, Miranda... it's okay. Look at me, Kitten." She opened her eyes, exhaled, and wanted nothing more than to melt into him, glowing. Drew released her hands and held her tight. When she met his gaze, he was watching her, loving her, and it was okay. They matched the rhythm of the water splashing on the shore below.

"You wanna know the best thing about having sex way out here at the boathouse?" She raised her eyebrows, assuming this was important enough to talk about right now. "Because out here in the boathouse, Miranda... *no one can hear you scream!"* He laughed a silly, evil laugh.

She tried to come up with something clever to say, something to let him know she wasn't scared or impressed. But there were no words... no time, only a pause… a catch in her breath. Her cheeks burned, lost somewhere in his fire. Glass was falling, crashing out of control. She tried not to scream and screamed anyway. Miranda was breathing hard, her body damp with sweat, his and her own. Drew moaned, a low, satisfied rumble, then fell quietly beside her, the two of them exhausted and weak on his flannel sheets. There would be no talk of cookies, or boats, or old luggage tonight. Drew got up and pulled on a pair of boxer shorts. He disappeared for a moment and came back with a broom, the blanket from the back of the couch, and a glass of water. He was so thoughtful. In many ways it was Miranda's first time.

"I'm sorry about your lamp, Drew. I must have bumped it. I don't know what happened." She was beaming.

"We both know exactly what happened." Drew put the water on her nightstand, and with a grin, asked her not to break it. He kissed her cheek and whispered in her ear, "It was that good for me, too."

The moon was nearly full and cast a pale light across her body, her hair a tousled mess on his pillow. He quickly swept up the glass on the floor. "I don't want you to get up and cut your feet, Kitten. I've heard all the screaming I can handle for one night." There was a train in the distance. Alfred Hitchcock was smiling, too.

Tonight there were no empty bottles to hide behind, no red lipstick to smooth the way. He didn't wonder if she loved him. Life was more complicated than one small word. He could not afford to deal with something as fragile as love, or Miranda's tender heart. Someday he would tell her everything, someday soon. It was about time for her to be honest with him, too.

Drew pulled the quilt up to her ears, threw the blanket on top. He would tease her about the lamp in the morning. The lake had smoothed out, all its ripples finally still, perhaps finding a moment of clarity. He watched her sleep, kissed her forehead, and whispered, "Goodnight, Kitten." Maybe tomorrow would be the day.

Tick tock

A very bad thing was about to happen. It's not like fate dropped this on her head, that she was forced to make a poor decision. What Miranda didn't know that morning, didn't realize as she slept quietly in Drew's arms, was that her next move would bring lasting consequence and despair.

Tick, tick, tick... Drew's alarm clock goes off at 7:30am. Daylight peeks through the window, Drew yawns, kisses her forehead, and gets up. Miranda is cold, wishes for her warm jammies and slippers. She settles for the NYU sweatshirt on the back of a chair and a giant pair of socks. Memories from last night linger— she's still tired.

Tick, tick, tick... The snooze alarm, louder than the first. Miranda smells bacon frying and remembers that she is starving. Drew is at the door, handsome, unshaven, wearing plaid boxer shorts. "Room service," he grins. The tray in his hands holds coffee, bacon, eggs, and a box of Krispy Kreme original glazed donuts, her favorite. He had been planning this all along.

He is clearly happy to see her there, tousled, and sleepy under the covers. Miranda smiles, one eye open. She and Drew, together at the boathouse, eating donuts after what might have been the most memorable night of her life. That very thought should have been a learning moment, a whack upside the head telling her she should forget about the list, her final date, and stay awhile. *Stay forever.*

Someone should have called, *GAME OVER!!...* should have sent out fancy announcements on fine stationary informing dates one through thirty that a winner had been chosen, and Miranda would live happily ever after in his sweatshirt, in his arms.

Drew thought her dating craze to find a husband was preposterous, simply a way for curious men to waste a lot of money on dinner with a girl who's not going to like them anyway. Drew knew exactly the kind of man she needed, and his name wasn't on any business card in a recipe box. He should have told her so.

"At least you'll have some stories to tell when you write your book someday." He was shouting over the sound of running water. "Some of those guys you went out with... where did you ever find a cartoonist? And the dentist who gave you the creeps? All this nonsense because of you and that stupid weed eater. I told ya, you should have called me."

Tick, tick, tick.... Yes, that would have been a good idea. But Miranda's foolishness and greed would once again lead her far away from the happy ending she longed for.

He turned off the water, stepped out of the shower. Wearing nothing but an old bath towel, Drew reappeared in the doorway with more coffee and a grin. But instead of following his lead and staying in bed, Miranda's mind wondered ahead to the business at hand. It was difficult to focus; intimacy was confusing. She was starting to unravel.

One mistake after another, sinking, falling, soon regretting. She was a plane crash in slow motion with no way to avoid the flames, the landing gear that failed, the crash that was about to happen. Miranda tiptoed away from Drew, the only man she ever really loved. There, she said it— but sadly, not out loud or to him.

A car door slammed in the lot below, the parts he had ordered were right on time. He was not independently wealthy, but had the work ethic of someone who deserved to be. Disappointed, he would be repairing the transmission on an old Chris Craft Cadette before she got out of the shower. While Miranda was still reliving the magic of last night, she was also aware of the time.

Tick, tick, tick... It was day 30. Just one more date to meet before she picked her new husband. Yes, last night may have thrown off her agenda a bit, because now her heart was involved in a plan that was intended to be strictly business. Maybe it was okay that Drew didn't have a lot of money, that he lived in a modest little place on the lake. How important was it to own a jet, or an island, or a shipping company in the Port of Miami? She walked past the Louis Vuitton trunk, too trapped inside her own thoughts to care.

Despite her true feelings and her longing to stay, she was determined to finally learn the identity of date #30, the mysterious D.W. Manos.

Seeking Miranda

Dominic Manos

Dominic Manos took the last sip of his martini and handed the glass back to Hanna. She was an excellent chef and an even better bartender. On board for the summer were Hanna, four handsome young deck hands, and Captain Daniel Bering at the helm, a picture of physical fitness, seamanship, and dashing good looks. The uniformed crew operated with seamless precision; the same performance Manos expected from everyone in his employ. He was looking forward to another summer in Traverse City. And he was looking forward to his date with Miranda.

Manos reached for his briefcase, pulled out a manila folder, and opened an envelope with her name on it. He was relaxing in the salon with a stack of newspapers, the Wall Street Journal on top. He would soon be making some changes to his portfolio, and decisions had to be made. He thought about re-lighting the cigar in the monogrammed ashtray, checked the time, then changed his mind. Manos smiled at the photograph of a girl in a red snow suit being hoisted up the mast of her dockmate's sailboat. He liked Miranda's sense of adventure, and wondered what she would be like in person... to know her intimately. He knew she drank too much, which suited him.

Keeping an eye on Miranda during her winter stay in Charlevoix was not just to satisfy his curiosity. Living aboard can be dangerous any time of the year. For a girl to be alone on the dock during a Michigan winter was unheard of! Maybe that was part of the allure. Of course, his intention was not motivated by personal gain or a desire to invade her privacy. His only concern was to provide help if she needed it— a nice hotel room, someone to shovel the walk, and financial assistance if necessary. And also, for no wrong reason, to keep track of the people she spent time with. It was a lengthy but necessary part of the screening process.

Another photo, and another. He liked the one of Miranda sawing long pieces of PVC pipe to build a complex superstructure. It was impressive. She couldn't have looked more elegant than she did the day at Saks in Palm Beach trying on David Yurman. She knew how to handle herself and do it with panache. He held up the picture from Deeny's the night that Miranda punched the guy who hit on her. It was a great photo. Manos had it blown up to 8 X 10, sure she would get a kick out of it when they went through all the pictures later.

Another photo showed her in the engine room of her boat, changing the oil, replacing a fuel filter, and cussing like a sailor when she bumped her head. Neil Lipman provided a complete report. He and Joe Ramono would be rewarded for their efforts. Manos was happy when Miranda landed the job with Jim Tiller. It was important that she was smart enough to fill the position he had in mind. Being lovely and feminine was essential, too. He was happy to see her determination to rise above the level of "trophy wife," a role she had played so well with Brian Parker Hall and Harry Stowe. Now, if things worked out— and he was confident they would— she wouldn't have to work another day in her life.

The surveillance reports arrived weekly at his winter home in Miami. Joe Ramono promised him a thorough and professional job, and delivered on his word. And while Manos initially had his doubts about Neil Lipman, Joe's brother-in-law came through with flying colors once he figured out how to work the little camera. Dominic checked his tie in the mirror, walked down the gangway, and headed for Petoskey. By now Miranda had dating down to a science. She had little hope that #30 was going to be anything special. For all she knew, D.W. Manos was just another guy she met at a bar. If not for that shiny gold business card, he would have been discarded with all the rest. After finally being with Drew, her heart just wasn't in it.

Miranda began her nightly routine, but with less enthusiasm than all the times before. She yawned, brushed her teeth, and went through the motions. She pulled out a little black dress from her collection, nice black stilettos from Nine West, and red lipstick— Revlon

Little Red Red, a moist, cheerful red that would last through dessert. She finished with a light spritz of Chanel No.5— the fragrance no longer inspired her. She was getting tired of the same old thing. She headed downstairs and spotted Drew's ball cap on the sofa. She held it up to her face, took a long, delicious breath, and stashed it behind a pillow. She missed him already.

Miranda would be glad when all this was over. She was sick of going on dates, tired of making small talk with boring strangers. Maybe it *was* a stupid way to find a husband. Maybe she didn't even *need* a husband. Surely, she could get another job, make her mortgage payment, and hire a kid to mow the lawn. *How hard could it be?* She was feeling hopeful, thinking about her future in a different way when the doorbell rang. Miranda peered through the old screen. Her face froze— she was speechless! She swallowed the last sip of scotch from a crystal rocks glass— part of a set she got from one wedding or another; she couldn't recall.

The man in the navy blue blazer was dapper and impeccably groomed. He looked the same as all those times they had almost, but never actually met. Miranda surmised that he must have as many blue blazers as she had little black dresses in her closet. Manos was tan and wore expensive shoes without socks— a sign that he was used to spending winters in a warmer place. Harry always loved nice shoes.

Miranda remembered looking into his eyes that first night at Tommy's Gotcha, blue as the sea, but tonight far from tranquil. She thought about sending Number 30 away before their date began, but decided it wasn't fair to judge. He *was* handsome and proper, and had that old money way about him. She recalled some familiar words of wisdom, Bible verses she wrote down and stuck to the refrigerator on her old boat. She had known too many fools, bitter strangers, and bad men to go back to her old ways now.

"Leave the presence of a fool, for there you do not find words of knowledge." Proverbs 14:7

"The heart knows its own bitterness and no stranger shares its joy." Proverbs 13: 10

"There is a way that seems right to a person, but its end is the way to death." Proverbs 13:12

Even so, inertia was luring Miranda down a familiar path, a tired stroll through a garden of shiny glass flowers, fake rocks, and weeds as smooth as velvet. It all felt so real, so full of life—a scene from her past she remembered well. She studied Manos, deciding whether she should open the door and let him come in or sneak out the back door and run! Oddly, there was a misplaced familiarity about this man that made her feel secure. In a way, he reminded her of Harry.

She thought about the years they were married, and the way he took care of her. It sure was nice not having to worry about money or anything else for that matter. Sometimes she missed her old life. She wanted to go shopping at Nordstrom and drink martinis at the club! Maybe taking care of herself was just too hard. She took a sip of scotch then it hit her. *How could I forget about that Louis Vuitton trunk at the boathouse?! Why am I standing here in a dress wasting time with this man? Have I lost my mind?* Was it a rhetorical question, or a taste of foreshadowing?

She decided she did not like men with manicured hands after all, or shoes that were too shiny. What she really liked were hands that were big and manly, strong enough to hold her the way she liked it. She knew she would rather climb on the back of Drew's motorcycle than go for a drive in the late model Mercedes parked in her driveway. Her life today was good, and yet, she was conflicted.

Miranda opened the door, wearing her most ladylike smile. The man in the navy blue blazer extended a manicured hand and said, "Dominic Manos. It's a pleasure to finally meet you, Miranda." She remembered the time she was paying for her magazines at the airport. He said her name in a familiar way, as if somehow, he already knew her. She pushed the uncomfortable memory aside and invited him in.

Manos carried yellow roses, a bottle of Merlot, and a bottle of Champagne, a signal that he was expecting a drink. Miranda went to the kitchen, poured a glass of wine and spilled the other. Her hands were shaking—perhaps too much coffee late in the day. She cleaned up the mess, convinced herself she was fine. She heard her own voice quietly say, *create an emergency! Fake a migraine! Just send him away while there is still time.*

Miranda returned to the living room, goblets in hand, to find Dominic Manos stalking the perimeter, inspecting her artwork as if he were in a proper gallery. He paused at a framed lithograph, a floral watercolor. The painting was all she had left of her dear orchids. Later she would find out that this, too, was part of the screening process— her good taste, attention to detail, her personal private world that Neil Lipman could not penetrate.

Miranda sat on her soft leather sofa while Dominic took a seat across from her in a vintage wing chair, one of the pieces she and Drew refinished on the weekends. D.W. Manos was smooth and refined— smiling on cue, cocking his head this way and that. While he charmed her with small talk, Miranda couldn't stop thinking about the times they almost met.

She recalled Manos sitting with the usual crowd at Tommy's Gotcha the night before she left for Charlevoix. Miranda recalled someone telling her to stay away from him, that he was not her type. She thought it was Vince, and wondered now what he meant by that. There was nothing overtly suspect about Dominic Manos that night, and in spite of a few mistakes along the way, Miranda considered herself an excellent judge of character, especially where men were concerned. She remembered having a scotch, kissing Tommy's cheek, and leaving the bar early. She recalled that everyone got real quiet. Maybe something happened after that? Miranda hoped they weren't talking about her.

She smiled in Dominic's direction, crossing her legs, leaning in and tilting her head this way and that. Manos took a sip of wine while Miranda drifted back into the cold mist of Castle Rouge. She remembered having a strange vision that night that carried her beyond the walls of the old stone warehouse, a place just beyond her reach.

All her old drinking buddies were there. She finished her wine and quietly stepped back into the vivid darkness to take a look around. One of the pirates said her name. She recognized the voice— IT WAS MANOS!! She knew it! Miranda squinted her eyes, looking deeper into the illusion. Did he really reach out and hand her a gold coin? How was that possible?

Miranda took a deep breath and drifted back to her living room where Dominic who was studying her blue swirl Millefiori vase. He asked whether she had traveled to Murano with Harry, or if she got it here in the states. She smiled a sincere smile and nodded the way rich people do when they're pretending to listen. Dominic's glass was still half full. He seemed perfectly content entertaining himself, so Miranda went back into Castle Rouge one last time.

Pirate extraordinaire Dominic Manos stood erect and proud, leaning against the old stone bar, watching Miranda, and toasting a handsome young man with chiseled features and neatly combed hair. His uniform had epaulets and an insignia on the chest pocket that said *Neptune's Hammer.*

She heard someone say her name; it startled her! Manos extended his hand, gave her his glass, and asked for a refill. He was wearing the ring!! It was carved with the trident, the insignia of Neptune, King of the Sea! He raised one eyebrow, looked up at her, and asked if everything was alright. Miranda walked to the kitchen, her tall black shoes click-clicking with trepidation.

Manos inspected her as if she were a nice pre-owned Porsche— low miles, glossy finish, full leather— used, but still desirable. Miranda wanted him to leave, but instead poured more wine. *How could the Bible verses on the refrigerator abandon her this way?* Manos raised his glass, grinned at his prey, and said, "Cheers." In the distance she heard pirates laughing.

On that fateful night, Miranda could tell that Manos was already in love. There was a certain dance, the mating ritual of wealthy men... the preening, the flattery, the verbal parading of one's fine material things. Men of means were predictable that way. It wasn't about hugs and kisses or dates to nice places (although he talked incessantly about his plane and his young Greek pilot). It was more about a fierce determination to close the deal, the sweat on the collar of his starched white shirt, and a predatory instinct to seize his prey quickly and without hesitation. She had been an intimate part of his life all these months, so from his vantage point, it was time.

They cruised Little Traverse Bay on his yacht and dined on a sumptuous dinner of Chateaubriand, garnished with happy, yellow nasturtiums. He was delighted that she knew about the tiny edible flowers, once again testing her level of refinement. When Hanna brought out Black Forest Oreo Pie for dessert, Miranda couldn't get over the coincidence. But then she remembered that Manos knew everything about her—cookies and all the rest.

She wondered if he knew about Charlie Fine... all the things she did with him. They wore the matching rings so there had to be a connection. Miranda looked at the dessert in front of her and thought of Drew. With every delicious bite, she felt her heart crumble.

Manos knew from countless audio tapes and photographs what she liked and what she did not. Otherwise, how would he know how to keep her satisfied when the time came? They shared a good laugh over a picture of Miranda walking across the football field at Ohio Stadium in high heels. He recalled a night when she was so beautifully dressed in Palm Beach, the night she stopped for a drink at Taboo. There would be spending sprees more fabulous than that if she accepted his offer, and Dominic was certain she would. Miranda could never resist temptation.

For all the nights she read her Bible and wanted to know the truth, she could never put down her shiny things long enough for the message to stick, much less find Jesus in those pages. He chuckled and grinned, pleased that his clandestine operation had been a success. Miranda was sipping scotch beside him on the sofa of the yacht's grand salon, waiting for photographs from Castle Rouge to surface next. So far there was nothing. She reminded herself that tonight's date was simply a formality. Number 30 was just the last move in a silly game of chess.

"I do not understand what I do. For what I want to do I do not do, but what I hate I do." Romans 7:15-20

Of special interest to Dominic Manos, was Miranda's weakness for alcohol. He knew from his sources at Tommy's and Jack's Steakhouse how much she liked to drink. All those years ago when she was married to Brian Parker Hall, she refused to heed the wisdom of Mavis Jackson, and even her trusted friend Lydia Peyton-Pierce could not convince her to stay with Alcoholics Anonymous long enough to make it stick.

That night on Dominic's boat, Miranda tried to stay focused. She maintained her resolve not to have another drink, until Dominic offered her a Macallan 15 year—rare, expensive, not too smoky. She had to admit, he was a wonderful host. But Miranda knew better than to break her two drink rule. The worst thing she could do was get drunk, pass out, and end up in bed with him.

Dominic however, hoped she *would* break her two drink limit, get drunk, and pass out on his boat. He wasn't especially interested in having sex with Miranda. He had heard all about that from Charlie Fine. Theirs would not be that type of marriage. Under certain circumstances he would allow Miranda to have sexual relationships with other men if that's what it took to keep her happy. He wasn't sentimental that way, and judging by her past, neither was she. The details would be discussed in the morning. She would stay in one of the staterooms and join him for brunch and champagne. Dominic leaned back in his chair, lit up a cigar, and grinned. He wondered if Drew Becker was waiting for her.

It was an unfortunate matter that Miranda slept with her lover for the first time the night before. All those silly feelings of romance were clouding her thoughts and distracting her from the important opportunity before her. Manos decided that Miranda's infatuation with the young boat mechanic had run its course. It wasn't meant to be, or as Tommy used to say— *bashert.* Miranda needed a man with an obscene amount of money to quench her appetite. Having a job and supporting herself was an interesting experiment, but not something she could live with forever. With his modest wages and humble home, Drew would never be enough. He could never keep up socially, never really satisfy her, at least not in the way she needed.

Manos sent Captain Daniel Bering to explain all this to her boyfriend. There would *not* be another romantic encounter at the boathouse. Miranda would *not* be coming back. As for the photographs from Miranda's night at Castle Rouge, they would remain forever hidden, strictly reserved for Dominic's private viewing.

Flight 1439

It was not that Drew intended to keep certain parts of his life from Miranda. There were things from his past. He just wanted to make sure the time was right.

Drew moved into the boathouse not long after Hank died. His parents had never accepted his choices. His deep affection for his grandfather was a source of their disappointment, too— though he never understood why. Even so, Drew always took the high road and tried to get along. They were, after all, his only family.

He recalled getting back to the boathouse around dinnertime. He had gotten an early start that morning and brought home a couple of nice trout. His lines were set just outside the Mallard Point Club well before dawn. It was the way his grandfather taught him. He used ice shavings on top of the hole to block out the morning sun. Fish were harder to catch if they got nervous. He put down his auger and ice scoop on the floor of the boathouse and took his keys from the hook. There would be time to put his tools away in the morning.

His parents were supposed to get home late that night. He would fillet himself a nice meal and take the other fish to his parent's cottage in the morning. They were due into Detroit after a late flight from LAX. Drew was babysitting his best boyhood friend, Missy the golden retriever.

The phone rang. Drew dropped an old spatula on the wooden floor; grease spattered. The voice on the other end sounded mechanical, as if they were reading from a carefully prepared script. Drew sat on the floor next to the dog. As he listened, the trout in the frying pan blackened and burned. It was not the only fire that night.

His parent's flight ran into some trouble, the voice explained. Seems that USAir flight 1439 landed and crashed into a commuter plane waiting on the same runway for take-off. The fire was almost instantaneous as the 737 dragged the helpless turbo prop beneath its flaming belly. The National Transportation Safety Board would later report that the fire originated in the forward cargo hold under the first-class cabin. Drew's parents were seated in seats 2A and 2B.

Drew would later learn that only three of the six exits were operational that night. The front exits were blocked by flames. There was chaos— the smoke was blinding. While 76 of the passengers escaped, 43 did not. Drew's parents died in the crash, presumably from asphyxiation. The NTSB findings concluded that the fuel from the crushed commuter flight combined with the

737's damaged oxygen system, was lethal. Drew was paralyzed with grief when he learned that his parents would never come home— that the rift between them would never be repaired.

And then there was the matter of the will. William Becker had business interests besides the Bridge Street Marina. Although they never talked much about business or his father's finances, Drew always wondered about his father's wealth, and just how it came to be. He was an only child— he would inherit everything. He was about to get some answers.

With his grandfather gone, Drew dealt with his sorrow alone. By now, he already had a respectable boat repair business, a HackerCraft of his own, and more than enough money to last a lifetime, but no one to share it with. He was sure that when the right person came along, he'd know her in an instant.

After his parents' death, seasons went by, but Drew's world stayed the same. He was withdrawn and remained close to home. It wasn't a good way to meet women. Entering a close relationship was a risk he could not afford to take— until that spring day when he kissed Miranda. Though he was smitten by her fiery spirit and sweet silly ways, he tried to keep his distance, at least where his heart was concerned. Maybe she was *the one.* He wondered if her drinking could lead to trouble, but his heart wouldn't listen. Drew decided to take a chance on Miranda.

A few summers earlier, Drew worked on several systems upgrades on *Neptune's Hammer,* the luxury yacht owned by Greek millionaire, Dominic Manos. Before he met Miranda, Drew installed a custom integrated bridge system, the most sophisticated navigation package of its kind. While the job required the utmost skill and experience, Manos treated him like a simple dock hand, a lackey who just got in the way.

Before the work was finished, Manos accused him of stealing parts. Drew walked off the job and never got paid. Miranda was so determined to complete her manic search for a husband, that warning her about Manos would have only piqued her curiosity more. There was no point in trying to control her; that much he knew. He was certain her "date" with Dominic would never amount to anything. Love was about making a choice, and he knew her heart belonged with him. He never told Miranda that he could buy and sell Dominic Manos many times over. True love was never about the money.

Drew worked twice as hard after the plane crash. Wood boats had feelings, and wood boats had hearts. As long as they were afloat there was life inside. The woodies listened in a way that no one else could. One Saturday afternoon, while Drew was sitting behind his shop enjoying a beer, something odd happened. It was October and the geese were in full migration, one of the prettiest times on the lake.

A small black squirrel was running in and out of the weeds along the gravel driveway, carrying small bits of paper. It appeared to be coming from his grandfather's old work truck, parked right in the spot where he left it. Drew smiled, sipped his beer, and watched. Nothing seemed out of the ordinary until he noticed more squirrels carrying paper, too! He sat quietly as they ran up the drainpipe and straight into the boathouse attic. Drew always enjoyed a good mystery. He didn't care if a few critters wanted to camp out at the boathouse this winter. Nights were long and lonely— he might even enjoy their company!

He ran inside, took the stairs two at a time, and pulled down the attic ladder. Sure enough, his suspicions were confirmed! It appeared as though the squirrels had been making their nest for some time! But when he took a closer look, they weren't building it out of paper at all— they were building it out of MONEY!! He flew down the stairs, ran across the driveway, and pulled back the weeds. He yanked hard on the door, and looked inside.

There were things that Drew did not know about his grandfather.

Hank Becker

Hank was a bear of a man, both tall and wide. He had a coarse gray beard, always neatly trimmed even in his older years, and wore a gold ring. He was a man who took pride in his appearance. His face was a map of deep lines and wrinkles, tracing all his journeys like a faded nautical chart. Even with his shiny eyes, sunny disposition, and all the times he worked on boats for free, some of the people in town were suspicious. Hank had no wife, yet one day showed up with a five-year-old son named, Billy. It was no secret that Hank Becker had girlfriends on every shore, and friendships with certain businessmen in Detroit. Drew understood that his grandfather used to travel on business, but that's all he knew. Hank didn't want Drew to know any details about his past until his grandson was old enough to understand. Hank Becker had a secret.

While still in his teens, Hank learned of a career opportunity on the water, a sales job of sorts. Seeing this as the adventure of a lifetime and a chance to make a positive difference in peoples' lives, he tuned up his boat and embarked on this new enterprise. Hank was admittedly a bit of a drinker. He was outraged at the passage of the 18th Amendment in the winter of 1920. Rather than just complain about the injustice of Prohibition, he vowed to fight the new law in his own private way.

Hank Becker already had the perfect boat. The newly designed 26-foot HackerCraft had a V-hull, a sleek design, and an aircraft engine that made it faster than any boat on the water. Hank was an ambitious young man. He made a few changes to the seating and upholstery, the space behind the dashboard, and the gas tank. With his mechanical skills, no one could keep up, and no one could stop him! That was the key to his success as Hank ran thousands of cases of English gin and French champagne down from Canada to Detroit, with a regular stop at Charlevoix. There was no shame in being a rum runner. He worked hard and made more money than he ever dreamed of. Life for Hank Becker was good.

There was a private late-night ship that ran from Lake Charlevoix to Boyne City where politicians, wealthy businessmen, and their "dates" could enjoy a cocktail or two. The boat was called the *Keuka,* a 75-foot party barge that entertained from nightfall until dawn. And that's where Hank met Hattie. In a way, Hank Becker was a businessman, too, and fit in well with the wealthy clients. Many became friends who helped him with his business affairs in later years. Hank always had plenty of cash for tips, but avoided keeping large sums of money on board. If for some reason he had to scuttle the Hacker to avoid being caught and arrested, he would not want his earnings to go down with the ship. However, he always brought generous amounts of liquor in exchange for a warm welcome. He was popular with the ladies.

Hattie was an Irish girl with pale skin and lips like a rose. She was Hank's regular date. When Hank stopped to see her, she greeted him with a kiss and a smile, secretly imagining how it would be to have a husband come home to her at night, a life with the man she loved. When they climbed into bed together, she pulled out the cheap jeweled pins from her hair, and shook loose her auburn curls. They felt soft and cool against his broad chest, his belly, his thighs. Hank always thought she looked like a girl from the country, or maybe a farm down state— so fresh and lovely, even without much make-up— so different than the other girls who entertained on board. If Hank were the marrying kind, which he was not, she was the kind of girl he would choose to be his wife.

Hattie listened to Hank Becker's stories, tales of his life as a kid growing up on the lake, and his plans to build a boathouse someday. It would be a place where he could work on boats by day, drink a few beers, and enjoy the sound of the lake at night. Hank and Hattie talked for hours. Running whiskey was only a means to an end— Prohibition couldn't go on forever, at least that's what his bosses on the dock were telling him. Hank was making a fortune, far more money than any one man would need in a lifetime. He stashed money everywhere, hoping that when the time came, he could find a safe place to hide it.

Maybe the tax collectors and revenuers wouldn't be too interested in a small-time businessman who lived a quiet life by himself, but Hank couldn't take any chances. The government was already doing enough to hurt the working man by closing the bars and taking away the alcohol. Hank Becker was damn sure they weren't gonna take a piece of him, too. Lucky for Hank, he had friends who had associates who knew how to take large sums of money, process it through a series of financial and business interests, and make even more. Though a slow, sometimes tedious process, he would eventually get all of his earnings, minus a service fee, and minus the tips the businessmen kept for helping him.

Hattie was poor, one of seven kids, and dreamed of a life better than her own. Hank always came bearing gifts, usually a nice piece a jewelry or a souvenir from his travels. Hattie liked Hank a lot, and the feeling was mutual. But Hank had work to do. His runs up and down the lake increased because demand was so high. He could not afford to let his bosses down. He saw her less and less. Then one rainy night he motored up to the dock, a wrapped present in his hand, and the girls said she was gone. They glared at him in an accusing way. One of them spit on his shoe. They thought he was more than just another wealthy man coming to the Keuka for sex. Hattie always thought he was special too, but things had changed.

Hank focused on his job. He was good at making runs in the dark, in the fog, and without port or starboard lights that would make him visible to another craft. Making deliveries in the worst conditions was an asset on the water, and allowed him to make late night trips that others would not dare. Being dependable made him popular with his clients, and the money kept pouring in, not just for the product, but in tips and bonuses, too. By now, Hank Becker knew the tricks of the trade. He learned how to use cans of old engine oil to pour on the hot exhaust manifolds in case he was in danger of being caught. Instantly, Hank could create a thick smoke screen to camouflage his location and make a quick getaway. Running hard is what he did. It was better to be safe than sorry.

Hattie's baby was born in the spring, and she loved her new role as a mother. She hadn't seen Hank in all those months, sure that he had lost interest by now. When she went back to work, she had a new client who was wealthy, charming, and kind— and he loved children! When he asked her to marry him, she accepted. She moved out of her family's small home just outside East Jordan, and moved into her husband's big house on Walloon Lake. There was no transportation to the neighboring towns, but her husband promised to take her. Months went by before she saw her family.

Hattie was surprised when her husband told her they would be spending the winter at his home in California. He suggested she leave the baby with her sister, just temporally until she got settled. She did not want to make him mad. Sometimes he had a bad temper when he drank. Hattie's family didn't have much money, but at least the boy would have plenty of love.

Her husband left Michigan before she did, boarding the luxurious passenger steamship, the "Northland," in Harbor Springs. Hattie stayed behind to button up the cottage, and would go to California a week later on the train out of Charlevoix. She was raised in the area and knew the schedules well. Traveling alone was not a concern. However, she wasn't sure how she was going to manage her heavy old trunk once she got there. Even though she found it at a church basement thrift store, and even though it was faded and tattered, it was her prized possession.

The day before her trip, Hattie got a ride to Charlevoix. She would stay one night at the hotel and take the early train in the morning. The driver placed the trunk on the sidewalk near the ticket window and wished her well. She could see a boathouse on the shore, just like the one Hank said he would build someday. His truck was parked at a single wooden dock down below. Hattie sat on a bench, spotted Hank, and watched him.

There were two boys swinging on a rope from a lamp post beside her. She offered them money to watch her things, half now and half later. She stood at the top of a grassy hill next to a diner that served breakfast all day. Hank was carrying a toolbox in one hand, and passing out candy to some boys with the other. She called out, "I hope you asked their moms if it's okay to eat that. Too much sugar's not good for children." She missed her son, a boy she called Billy.

Hank looked up, the sun in his eyes. She took off her shoes and carried them down the hill, her heart racing. When Hank saw her, he could not speak, just threw open his arms and held her tight. It had been almost five years. Hattie sat down in the grass, and Hank walked up the hill to tip the boys and retrieve her things. They loaded up the Hacker and motored to the boathouse, making polite but awkward conversation along the way. Hank had heard she got married. Hattie spent the night with him, knowing it would be the last time. She woke up late, got distracted, and lingered in bed with Hank a while longer, just as they had done years ago. She dried her tears and gathered up her things, leaving behind her trunk in her haste. Hank got out of his truck at the train station and walked with her. The conductor said they made such a nice couple. Hank passed the man his Kodak box camera and asked him to take their picture. And then she told him about his son.

Any man who could run whiskey all night and never get caught could certainly ask a few questions and find a boy in East Jordan. By the time Hank caught up with him, there were so many kids, grandkids, and strangers living in that tiny house, that no one had a problem letting the boy's dad take him home. Billy liked the water but was much more interested in school and books. He got good grades and made the honor roll. Now known only as William, he studied business and economics at New York University, opened his own firm, and eventually developed Hank Becker's original boat dock into a full-service marina. Of all his projects, this was his baby, the jewel of Michigan's west coast... The Bridge Street Marina. To the locals, it was simply known as the Boat Basin.

With Hattie on a train to California, there was only one complication from Hank's night with his girl. It was the matter of the old brown trunk. Hattie was gone; he was not likely to see her again. But Hank wasn't too concerned. Her drunken SOB of a husband was rich enough to buy her ten new trunks if she wanted! Hank would keep the trunk forever.

Windfall

Drew yanked open the door on the driver's side; a mouse scurried across the faded seat…

Then all at once he saw
that there was money in the truck!
He took the stairs two by two
and saw he was in luck! There was
money in the ceiling,
there was cash beneath the floor,..
he reached up high and found
that there were bills inside the door!
The cabinets and drawers had
secret cubbyholes inside,
though this was kept a secret
until the old man died.
The currency was everywhere,
a row of mason jars,

a bookshelf and a painting
by a young Pierre Bittar.

But who would hide a fortune
in a sofa made of leather?
The only answer Drew could find
was crafty old Hank Becker.
He took a breath to calm himself,
a windfall to his name,
could change his life and how he lived,
or keep it all the same.
He grinned and laughed and got a beer,
excited and perplexed,
then watched a squirrel go by and wondered
what might happen next.
The picture of the HackerCraft
was hiding money, too,
a note inside said Grandson,
this is all from me to you.

The Letter

Drew opened the envelope and immediately recognized his grandfather's scribbled hand.

By now I guess you've settled in at the boathouse and are taking good care of my old customers, just as we planned. It's a wonderful life, Drew... I know you'll love this place just as I have. There are some things about your family, Drew... things that I want you to know. There was once a lady in my life named Hattie. The last time I saw her... Well, that was a long story, a very long time ago. The old trunk in the living room is very special to me, not only because of what's in it, but because it belonged to her. She was the love of my life, son. She was your grandmother. If you found this letter, I assume you've discovered your fortune, my life savings, the earnings of my hard work. My career, as it were.

When you open the trunk, just remember I love you. And your grandmother loved you, too... She did. In case you haven't figured it out, the key to the trunk is on the hook by the door, the same place I always kept it. All this is yours.

One last thing. When you meet the right girl, Drew, follow your heart... don't ever let her go. If a man can ever learn from his grandfather's mistakes, remember this one thing.

Drew emptied his pockets. When he moved into the boathouse, he gathered up all the keys on all the hooks and put them on one ring so nothing would get lost. *The key to the trunk was with him all along.*

It took some jiggling to get the key in the lock. Time, inactivity, and moisture had taken their toll— he was careful not to force it. When he finally pried open the lid, the first thing that caught his eye was a shoe box full of treasures Hank had been saving all those years— the ball they caught at his first Tiger's game, some old fishing lures, and the booklet from the first time he took Drew to Hessell. There were photos, too... the day Drew got his mini-bike, the two of them in the Hacker holding a best in show trophy, and at least a dozen pictures of them fishing together.

There was a crumpled blue ribbon with a gold seal. Drew had completely forgotten that he was the seventh grade spelling bee champion! There was a picture of Drew dressed in a light blue tuxedo standing beside a girl in a formal gown and wearing a corsage... a prom date he could not remember. All of his report cards were there bundled together. Except for a formal wedding picture, Drew's parents were conspicuously absent from the happiest times in his life. Learning the truth about

Hank and Hattie explained a lot about his father's disdain.

The box full of memories and the news about his grandmother were all that mattered now. As a young man barely out of his teens, he didn't need any treasure beyond that. However, beneath the shoe box and a stack of old newspapers, there was more money! There were bills in neat piles held together by rubber bands, and money carelessly tossed in as though Hank had to put it there in a hurry. There was money he didn't even recognize, bills that looked old and faded worth $10,000 each! He didn't recognize the picture of the man on the front, a man named Chase. It looked like Monopoly money! Drew wondered if it was real, especially since there were stacks of them!

There were envelopes with notes on them and keys inside. From the looks of things, Hank had money stashed all over northern Michigan, clear up to Mackinaw City, down to Saginaw, and small towns in between that nobody ever visits— all places where a boat mechanic in dirty Levi's would fit right in with the locals.

But there was more! There were gold bars, gold coins, and precious gems wrapped in paper, just tossed into the trunk like the money! It looked like a treasure chest and a pirate's bounty! He could only stare into the open trunk and wonder how in the world his grandfather got all this. Did his parents know? As much as they disliked the old man, Drew wondered if it was his grandfather's money that had made them rich, too.

There was always talk about old Hank Becker around town. Drew didn't care what they said, figured they were just jealous. He wondered if he'd ever know the whole story. Drew decided it just didn't matter.

Seeking Miranda

Miranda greeted the man at the farmers market. August was tourist season, a busy month on the island. A gray-haired woman sat sleeping in a folding chair, a scarf tied loosely around her head, the ground dusty beneath her feet. Plastic bins of figs, peaches, and eggplant tempted curious travelers, while spirited twin boys escaped their parents' grasp and sent a tower of watermelons tumbling. There was no place more beautiful than Santorini, the most celebrated of all the Greek islands, the place Miranda would now call home.

It had been just over a year since Miranda married Dominic Manos. The wedding was a small private affair, attended only by Dominic's family and a few close friends. It all happened on such short notice that she could not send out invitations, much less expect anyone to buy a ticket and fly to Greece. Dominic said that was unfortunate, and promised her a trip back to the states soon. Miranda knew better than to complain.

They did a lot of traveling that first year. Dominic's Miami home was the address on his business card, the same place Joe Ramono sent the monthly reports about her. While the house was richly appointed and architecturally interesting, it felt lifeless and cold. It was only visited by the cleaning lady every Wednesday to dust, vacuum, and let in the pool man. It was featured on the cover of Miami Living Magazine right after it was built. He called it his pride and joy.

Dominic had always wintered in Miami alone. Miranda thought it was strange that he had never been married. But with a business to run, meetings with his associates, and ongoing projects to oversee, it should have been no surprise— she admired his work ethic. With a stack of new credit cards, she spent her days shopping in boutiques, drinking coffee, and trying to fit in. Miranda was drinking again, more than before, and didn't have the body she used to. South Beach dresses were for skinny young girls. Dominic assured her she would grow to love Miami.

In the summer they lived aboard *Neptune's Hammer* at Mallard Point. Miranda was happiest when she was in Michigan, full of fond memories of living on her boat, working for Tiller, and her much simpler life there. But with her former friends at Mallard Point looking on, she knew she was being scrutinized, even judged! It was not the homecoming she thought it would be, and it didn't help that Dominic Manos was not popular with her old crowd. She knew better than to ask the locals about

Drew Becker, certain there would be consequences for them both.

No one seemed to have much use for a girl who once cheated on her adoring husband, wreaking emotional havoc among the couples who were true to their marriage vows. Miranda was a reminder that no loving union was secure. Their thoughts were with Harry Stowe, his young bride, and the crash that killed them both. Even Charlie Fine looked away.

An hour south of Traverse City in Manistee, there was an exclusive club where Dominic met up with friends to go hunting. It was expensive to join— he was a lifetime member. He assured Miranda that hunting was a gentlemanly sport steeped in tradition, and that the animals were shot and processed in the most humane way. Miranda remembered the morning she watched a man in a golf cart pull a huge dead deer by a chain to an outbuilding where the processing was done. The animal's back legs were tied together, it was hoisted up on a large hook, and its belly slashed to let all the blood drain out. A young black lab eagerly licked up the mess—Miranda was repulsed.

There were rarely any other women staying at the lodge, and Miranda was left in the old kitchen where a chain smoker named Sergei prepared the evening meal. His specialty was venison meat pie. He snacked on small bits of pickled herring and onion while he worked; Miranda always declined. Rocks glasses were lined up in the freezer next to a bottle of vodka. Between sips he tapped his ashes in the stew and bored Miranda with the details of his young life in Russia. Sergei hated America. *Living in the U.S. was no life at all,* he used to say in a thick, angry accent. She watched in disbelief as he breasted out a full bucket of mourning doves, their feathered bodies still warm, their bones cracking softly. After dinner, the three of them emptied a bottle of Stoli. And instead of going to bed with his wife, Dominic slept with Sergei.

Miranda left Michigan and returned to Greece with her husband and a heavy heart. She devoted herself to learning the culture, getting to know Dominic's extended family, and enjoying her magnificent home. Her husband doted on her, filling her dressing room with many beautiful things. There were built in cases to display her shoes and handbags, much nicer than the old antique shelf she had in Petoskey. Dominic was proud to have her on his arm at every social affair, and his friends always said what a beautiful wife he had. Miranda switched from Stoli to scotch and only drank after five.

Despite his unflattering behavior that first night on the boat, the man she chose as her husband, the man who revealed photos, documentation, and secrets about her private life, had little appeal except his wealth— she knew it from the start. But Dominic Manos was a man of power and success. He had his reputation to consider, and she respected him for that. Manos was lucky number 30— he played the game and won, as did she.

Even so, Miranda was consumed with a deep longing, an undeniable sorrow and despair. She would stay in her dressing room, hiding from Dominic, hiding from her heart. Even with a view of the Aegean Sea, she really just wanted to go home. Miranda closed her eyes and watched the memories of that night with Drew... kissing, teasing, and a broken lamp— the life she left behind. The ladies in the Tarkay would have loved that story, especially the pretty one. Dominic promised the painting would follow her to Greece, but later decided a fresh start was better— the Tarkay was left behind.

The blue waters of the Mediterranean were like Dominic's eyes— placid one day, raging the next. Shades of cobalt, crimson, and gold swept the evening sky. But even with the island's immense beauty, she never stopped thinking about Lake Michigan... Jim Tiller, the snow at the Boat Basin, her dock mates, and springtime when it finally arrived. Miranda wept. Piles of wadded up Kleenex covered her dressing table. Even her new orchids, all lined up in a row, couldn't ease her pain. What she would not give to climb the stairs at the boathouse one more time... to fall asleep in his arms, to feel his lips on her cheek and whisper, *Good night, Kitten.* While her flowers were blooming, Miranda was dying inside. She wondered if Drew had met someone...

Miranda blew her nose and tossed another Kleenex into the pile. Dominic did not like it when she cried. There were nights when he drank too much. Sometimes she'd hear him pounding on the door demanding she come out and join him. Once he grabbed her by the arm and she tripped over a table. Even though it was an accident, she hated the bruises that were left behind. He never apologized, but bought her expensive jewelry whenever it happened; she was accumulating quite a collection.

Miranda didn't expect God to bail her out this time. With all that had gone on— her drinking, that night at Castle Rouge, the affair with Charlie Fine— maybe she was getting what she deserved. Miranda was certain God had written her off as a lost cause. Besides, Dominic hated it when she read her Bible. The small white book was now worn at the edges, the pages full of post-it notes and writing in the margins. The gold letters on the cover that once delighted her, had faded and gone. For all the nights she spent hiding from her husband, she might find some strength in reading it now. Miranda reconsidered. Maybe God was still there.

"Be strong and courageous. Do not be afraid or terrified because of them, for the Lord your God goes with you; he will never leave you or forsake you." Deuteronomy 31:6

Miranda took off her pretty sandals, strolled lazily along the beach, the black sand warm beneath her feet. She kicked a pebble along the way, the stones reflecting her sullen mood. Five thousand miles away, Drew kicked off his shoes and climbed the steps of the boathouse. He lived alone, no one to share it with.

Miranda looked up at her home, an impressive oceanfront castle on the highest cliff. There was a pool, a garden path, and a statue. There were vast rooms, a spiral staircase, and turrets. It was a masterpiece, even among the finest properties. But Miranda was alone—she kept going back to the same place.

She should have told Drew how much she really loved him. . . that his voice on the phone, his hands on her body, his smile, her goosebumps... it was all she wanted, all she needed! So much had changed! All the shoes and money and handbags in the world left her empty inside. The only riches that mattered now were in her heart... the place where only Drew belonged. She should have told him. Miranda walked along, her eyes filling with tears, her cheeks burning with shame and regret.

Drew knew Miranda loved him; that was no secret. Even though a year had passed, he missed her. He knew where she really belonged, yet hoped she was finally happy. Had he told her about his inheritance and his grandfather's money, he was certain she would have chosen him for the right reason, for the man that he was. All she really wanted from him was his heart, a midnight snack, and a ride on his motorcycle. She was easy to love— his wealth would not have mattered, he was sure. In the letter, his grandfather told him when he found the right girl, don't ever let her go. But he had. Drew was no stranger to loss. He would go on. Without her.

The sun came out and warmed her face, somewhat lifting her dark mood. She would greet Dominic with a hug, a kiss, and a lively story about her day. In time, her marriage would improve, she was sure of it. She looked to the sea and dried her tears. Miranda put on her husband's favorite smile, almost convincing herself. There was a familiar breeze, a train in the distance. She pulled a soft, ripe peach out of her basket, took a bite, and frowned. *It was bitter.*